PRAISE F
No Certain

"Lehrer raises thought-provoking questions. . . . [He] teases the mind with clever manipulations of narrative structure."
—*The Washington Post*

"A clever forensic mystery."　　　　　—*Publishers Weekly*

"[*No Certain Rest* is] meticulously researched and engagingly written. The characters are so well drawn, their pursuits and dilemmas so enticingly presented, that they provide full value just as characters."　　　　—*New York Daily News*

"*No Certain Rest* has a good heart, and its puzzles make good reading for a rainy day."　　　　—*Seattle Post-Intelligencer*

"Lehrer, who writes simple, straightforward prose and moves his story along rapidly . . . is at his best in conveying the passion Civil War students feel for their subject, the empathy they feel for the war's soldiers, the thrill they get when research reveals enough pieces to solve a historical puzzle. . . . Civil War devotees will join murder mystery fans in enjoying *No Certain Rest.*"
—*Providence Journal*

"Lehrer does a remarkable job of making the reader feel what it must have been like to fight at Burnside Bridge. . . . [The descriptions] are so real that one feels compelled to visit the site. . . . [The images] remain with the reader long after finishing the book."
—*Legal Times*

ABOUT THE AUTHOR

No Certain Rest is JIM LEHRER's thirteenth novel. He has also written two memoirs and three plays. The executive editor and anchor of *The NewsHour with Jim Lehrer* on PBS, he lives with his wife, Kate, in Washington, D.C. They have three daughters.

ALSO BY JIM LEHRER

Viva Max!

We Were Dreamers

Kick the Can

Crown Oklahoma

The Sooner Spy

Lost and Found

Short List

A Bus of My Own

Blue Hearts

Fine Lines

The Last Debate

White Widow

Purple Dots

The Special Prisoner

NO
CERTAIN
REST

RANDOM HOUSE TRADE PAPERBACKS / NEW YORK

NO
CERTAIN
REST

A NOVEL

Jim Lehrer

2003 Random House Trade Paperback Edition

Copyright © 2002 by Jim Lehrer

Map copyright © 2002 by David Lindroth, Inc.

All rights reserved under International and Pan-American Copyright Conventions. Published in the United States by Random House Trade Paperbacks, a division of Random House, Inc., New York, and simultaneously in Canada by Random House of Canada Limited, Toronto.

RANDOM HOUSE TRADE PAPERBACKS and colophon are trademarks of Random House, Inc.

This work was originally published in hardcover by Random House, Inc., in 2002.

Library of Congress Cataloging-in-Publication Data
Lehrer, James.
No certain rest: a novel / Jim Lehrer
p.   cm.
ISBN 0-8129-6822-0
1. Archeologists—Fiction.   2. Antietam National Battlefield (Md.)—Fiction.
3. Antietam, Battle of, Md., 1862—Fiction.   I. Title.
PS3562.E4419 N6 2002   813'.54—dc21   2002075177

Printed in the United States of America
Random House website address: www.atrandom.com
2 4 6 8 9 7 5 3 1

Title-page photo by Jim Lehrer
Book design by Victoria Wong

To Timothy Seldes

Battles such as the one fought on this ground are never really over. The force of the collision and the rawness of the death and the loudness of the screams preclude certain rest. We will always be called upon from time to time to deal with the remains from what happened here.

—Gary Wayne Doleman, Colonel, U.S. Army (Ret.)

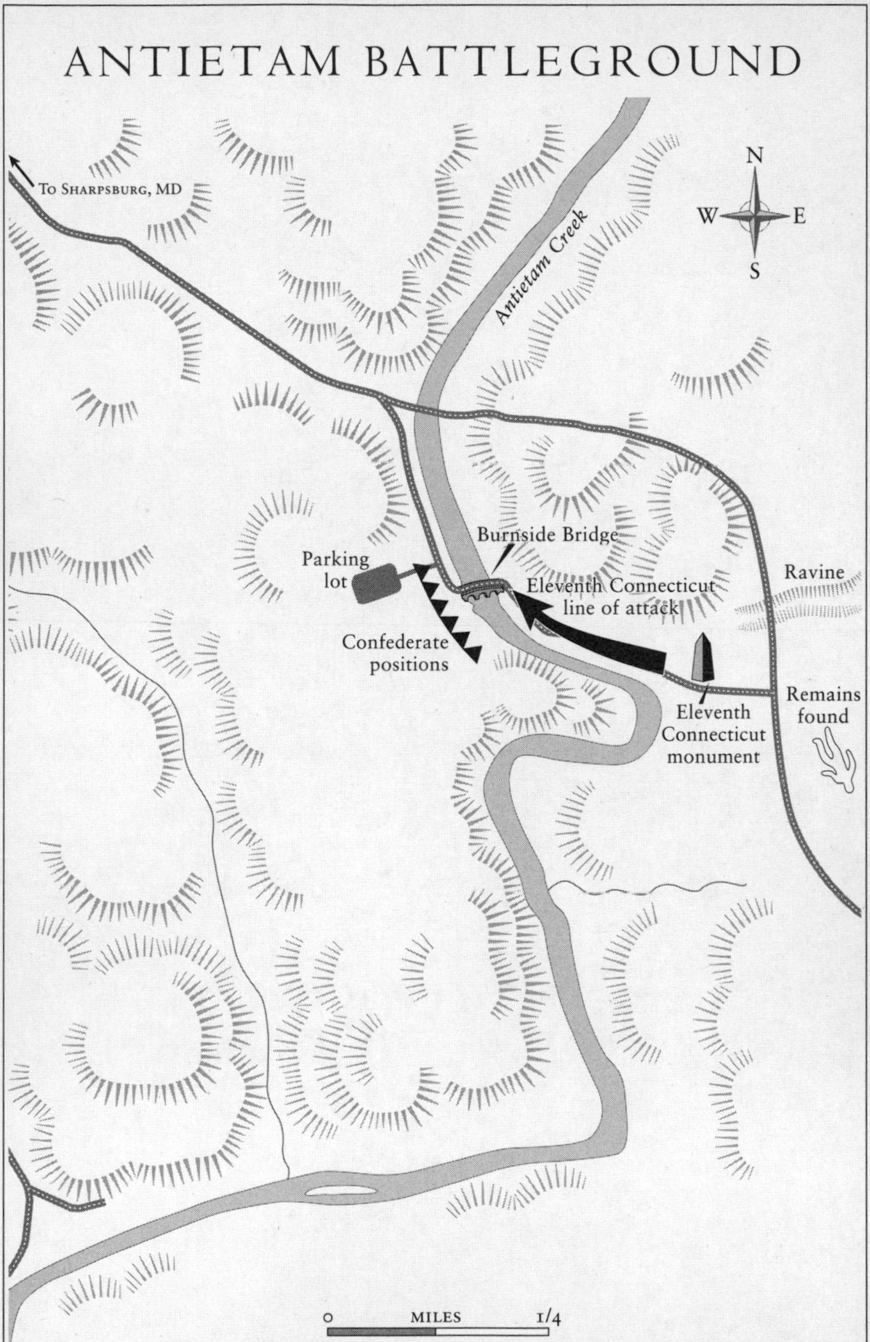

ANTIETAM BATTLEGROUND

To Sharpsburg, MD

Antietam Creek

N
W E
S

Burnside Bridge

Parking lot

Eleventh Connecticut line of attack

Confederate positions

Ravine

Eleventh Connecticut monument

Remains found

0   MILES   1/4

PART ONE

REMAINS

I

She said she would be the short, dumpy blond woman carrying a thin, green leather valise. He told her he would be the tall, skinny man wearing rimless glasses and an Indiana Jones fedora.

There she was. There was Rebecca Fentress of the Marion County, Iowa, Historical Society. And here he was, Don Spaniel of the National Park Service. He had guessed, from the sound of her voice on the phone, that she could be somewhat elderly, as old as seventy possibly. But fifty-five or even less was his best estimate now upon seeing her in person. Not only did she talk older than she was, she was dressed that way in a two-piece dark blue cotton dress with a skirt that fell a good two inches below the knee.

"Doctor Spaniel, I presume," she said to him.

"Ms. Fentress?" he said, removing his hat.

A friend had given him the fedora two years ago as a thirty-fifth birthday present. It was meant as a joke because Don, like Indiana Jones, was an archeologist. But Don so loved the hat that he had made it part of who he was, wearing it routinely. Reg Womach, his laid-back Smithsonian anthropologist friend, often called him Harrison, as in Harrison Ford, the actor who played Indiana

Jones in the movies. That didn't bother Don. He figured there were worse things in life for a skinny guy in glasses to be called than Harrison Ford.

"I have always wanted to say something like 'Doctor Spaniel, I presume,' " Ms. Fentress said.

Don Spaniel smiled at her. His impression was that here was a woman who was as pleasant as she was plain and who most probably, in his instant analysis, was very smart. He was prepared to like and admire her even more if the private Civil War papers of the late Albert Randolph of the Eleventh Connecticut Volunteers were in that green case she was clutching to her body.

They were standing just inside the main entrance of Washington's majestic Union Station—a six-foot-four gawky man leaning down to a speak to a five-foot-four solid woman who was looking almost straight up. In silhouette, they could have easily passed for a Norman Rockwell painting, possibly a small-town high school English teacher speaking to the basketball coach about a star player's D− theme on a Charles Dickens novel.

Rebecca Fentress had called Don from Union Station less than twenty minutes earlier to announce her surprise arrival in Washington, D.C., and to arrange an immediate meeting with him. He had suggested she get in a taxi and come to his office, which he assured her was barely ten minutes away in an area called Potomac Park. She said she really would rather not leave the station. All right, he said. How about meeting me in front of the huge electronic schedule board at the main entrance of the train station?

It was three in the afternoon. There were many people going to and from trains and milling about the many shops in Union Station, which had been very successful since being rehabilitated into a retail center as well as a train station a few years ago. He noticed the several open restaurants there in the main rotunda were not crowded and he suggested they find a quiet place in one.

"I don't fly on airplanes," Ms. Fentress said to Don. "It takes a long time to get from Iowa to here by train, it really does. You have to go through Chicago, for one thing; Pittsburgh, for another."

Soon, they were seated in the quietest corner of a place which, according to its menu, offered at least one food specialty from each of the fifty states.

"I'll bet the one from Iowa has something to do with corn," said Rebecca Fentress. "Corn is what people think of when they think of Iowa—corn and pigs." She was right. Iowa's representative was listed under side orders: corn on the cob.

She ordered a piece of pecan meringue pie, a specialty of New Mexico, and a cup of Maryland coffee, which appeared to Don to be like any other kind of coffee.

He didn't want anything now except what might be in Ms. Fentress's valise, but, to be polite, he got a simple no-state's Diet Coke.

"I have brought you Xerox copies of the Albert Randolph materials," Ms. Fentress said before she made even a move to touch anything.

Don wanted to reach across the table and hug Rebecca Fentress. But all he did—all he thought that was appropriate to do— was say, "Thank you very much. I really do appreciate what you have done." He came close to speaking on behalf of some long-dead men from a Connecticut regiment of volunteers with names such as Kingsbury, Griswold, Allbritten, and Mackenzie. But he thought better of it. That, too, would have been over the top.

"The originals are under lock and key at our local bank, and there they will likely always remain," she said. "No one will ever again be allowed to read them."

Don, in his state of hyperhappiness, didn't quite get it. What was she saying? "Why? What's the problem?" he asked.

"The problem is only that the board of trustees of our historical society decided our purpose was only to collect and preserve things from the past, not to stir them up."

She was no longer smiling as she took several bites of her pie and a sip of coffee.

"How do you plan to use the information contained in these papers, doctor?" she then asked.

"I'm not sure, to tell you the absolute truth. I am not sure, of course, what is in them to begin with. . . ."

"I told you on the phone that they were sensitive and that they were definitive. I am confident you will find them so as well. They will undoubtedly clear up any questions you might have about what happened at the bridge at Antietam on September 17, 1862."

"I'm delighted and excited at that prospect." *Delighted and excited* said only half of it. His very soul swung and swayed with the prospect of finally knowing exactly what had happened.

She pushed away her pie plate and coffee cup and reached over to her green case, which she had placed on the table to her left. She moved it in front of her and zipped it open.

Don Spaniel began to feel as if he were some kind of mysterious operative, here amid the cover of a crowded train station, receiving from Courier Fentress of Iowa the secrets, the goods—the magic.

"Here," she said, handing him a sealed white envelope. It looked thick. There were several pages of something inside.

Don took the envelope and said, "Thank you, Ms. Fentress. I promise you that I will not—"

"No promises, please. None is necessary. I did this of my own free will to satisfy my own needs and beliefs."

She zipped the valise closed, looked at her watch, and stood. "Now I must go catch my train."

Don was on his feet. "Where are you going?"

"Home, doctor. Home."

"But didn't you just get here?"

"I came here to hand you that envelope personally. I felt it was too important to leave to the vagaries of the U.S. mails or one of the private express firms. My mission accomplished, I am going home."

Don left a ten-dollar bill on the table. She started walking; he fell in beside her.

"Your luggage? Where is your luggage?"

"A redcap took it when I got off the train. He's probably now, as we speak, putting it in my compartment on the new train. That is what I asked him to do, at least. I love traveling in those bedrooms. Have you ever done that?"

"No, ma'am, I haven't."

"It's tight for two—are there two of you?"

"No, ma'am. And at the rate I'm going there may never be more than me—than one."

"There are worse things," she said with a clip in her tone.

Message most definitely received, Don said, "My problem is that my job is pretty much my life—too much, say the women who come and go. I'm accused of living too much in the past."

"That's what some people say about me, too."

They passed a boutique hardware shop and a bookstore and a model-train emporium and several more eating places and were now nearing her gate for Amtrak's Capitol Limited to Pittsburgh and Chicago.

He told her how much he had enjoyed meeting her, again thanked her, and again praised her for what she had done to help him resolve a 134-year-old mystery.

"It must be quite satisfying and fulfilling work you do as an archeologist, particularly on the Civil War."

"Extraordinarily so, yes, ma'am."

Ms. Fentress extended her right hand, and he took it in his. She said, "What I do is also satisfying and fulfilling. Few people at home understand why I would be content to run a historical society in my small town. I, frankly, can no longer imagine not doing so."

"I'm the same exact way," Don said.

She had more to say: "Please let me know once you have decided what you're going to do with the Randolph material."

Don promised to do so. He was suddenly eager for Rebecca Fentress to get back on her train. He wanted desperately to tear open the envelope and read the Randolph papers. Onward, please. Good-bye. Have a nice train trip, please. . . .

But there was one last thing. "Doctor Spaniel, I trust you are prepared to deal with the consequences of telling Albert Randolph's Antietam story?"

"I believe I am. . . . Yes, ma'am." It was, in fact, something to which he had not given that much thought. Most of what he had considered thus far had to do specifically with Jim Allbritten and Fred Mackenzie, two present-day descendants of the men in Randolph's story. But first, he had to confirm conclusively what had occurred in the heat of battle on an Antietam hillside 134 years ago. Then he would deal with what to do about it—what to say to Allbritten and Mackenzie, among others.

"Opening up graves can sometimes lead to an unleashing of old demons and to unexpected consequences," added Ms. Fentress.

"I know. Yes, I know," said Don, barely able to conceal his readiness for her to leave. But he owed her an answer. "I believe that those consequences, whatever they are, are part of the history. Whatever is meant to be, will be."

She seemed about to respond but then apparently thought better of it and did finally go.

But from the way she flicked her head to the right and squinted her eyes, Don read a message of disagreement from Rebecca Fentress of Iowa.

Whatever. Don watched with great pleasure as she showed her Amtrak ticket to the gate attendant and then disappeared in the direction of Iowa.

He spotted a section of deserted chairs by a train gate not then in use and raced for them, ripping open the envelope as he ran.

Once seated, he carefully removed the papers.

The first page was typed. It appeared to be a list of items, signed by a sheriff. Then there were an official army document, a copy of a newspaper clipping, a black-and-white photograph, and, finally, several pieces of white copy paper folded over in thirds and held together at the top by a large silver paper clip.

Don unfolded the pages. There was handwriting on them. It was a letter. He removed the clip.

He could feel his heart beating, his pulse quickening, his breath shortening—his soul leaping.

The handwriting was large, clear, and clean.

In the upper-right-hand corner of page one, in neat script, was the date. *"September Seventeen, Eighteen Hundred and Seventy Two."*

Ten years to the day after the battle of Antietam!

Then Don began to read the text:

I, Albert Randolph, here now render terrible words of confession. I have addressed them to no particular person or persons because I do not know who will ultimately read them. I have written them mostly for myself rather than for others. I have written them because I have no choice but to write them; my troubled soul and my angry God permit no other course.

I was party to one of the most heinous crimes the darkest side of the human spirit can generate. It was committed on a day ten years ago near a Maryland town named Sharpsburg on a creek called the Antietam.

I render this confession on this day because the anniversary memories are acutely painful to my being. That pain, unbearable and unrelenting, provides the force that moves my pen across this page.

On that morning of September seventeen, the year of our Lord eighteen hundred and sixty-two, I was serving as a sergeant in the Eleventh Connecticut Volunteer Regiment. Assigned to the Second Brigade of the Third Division of the Ninth Corps of the Army of the Potomac, we were a proud and worthy unit of men, dedicated to fighting for the preservation of our hallowed Union and for the glory and reputation of our beloved birth state of Connecticut.

We were on that day given the mission of seizing access to and control of the Lower Bridge across Antietam Creek, which was in the State of Maryland not far from the Potomac River and the State of Virginia. We were part of a large and determined force under the leadership of General George McClellan that had as its ultimate mission to destroy the Army of Northern Virginia under the command of General Robert E. Lee.

There were no questions in any mind or heart among those of us in the Army of the Potomac that we would be victorious.

Our regiment was made up of young men recruited from towns far and wide all over Connecticut after first being rallied by the governor and other politicians enraged by the Confederates' declaration of independence. We were keen on showing Connecticut's anger and its willingness to fight and to punish the wrongdoers and keep the Union together.

My own decision to follow my anger into the army of the

United States was influenced greatly by Roland Mackenzie and Kenneth Allbritten, two fierce patriots from our town of East Preston. When the war was over, Roland returned with me to East Preston.

Kenneth, may he rest in peace, did not.

It is the story of the three of us and others that I must now tell.

2

Don Spaniel's Antietam burden, like Albert Randolph's, grew from events that occurred on a hillside near the Maryland town named Sharpsburg, on a creek called the Antietam.

It was a Sunday in late May when two local Civil War relic hunters, Henry Milliken and Larry Samuels, were walking up and down the hills and through the fields and gullies and thorny patches of the twelve acres that made up Thaddeus Farm. In five hours of scouring the land with metal detectors, they had found only a few bullets and a small piece of red clay glazed black on one side. Henry knew enough about household items such as plates, vases, and pots to believe that the three-inch-square ragged hunk of baked clay was from the Civil War period. But there was no way to connect it directly to that struggle across the road at Burnside Bridge.

Both men, who were in their early forties, had grown up very much aware of the bloodshed at Burnside, but Henry was an expert. He knew as much about Civil War uniforms, buttons, weapons, bullets, and cannonballs as anyone in the Sharpsburg area. But Larry, office manager for a butane delivery company, told everyone he went hunting for Civil War relics mostly because it got him outside. And who knows, maybe I'll strike it rich, he joked.

Henry was a dedicated enthusiast who owned and operated a Civil War book and artifacts store and art gallery in Sharpsburg that specialized in the battle of Antietam. In just the past year, he had also become a reenactor, part of a group of forty-seven men from the Hagerstown-Sharpsburg area who, on anniversaries and special occasions, re-created the various skirmishes and events that made up that bloody day. Henry and the others equipped and uniformed themselves authentically as Union and Confederate soldiers, right down to their underwear and the food they ate.

Coming to this particular piece of land on this Sunday was a major event for Henry. He had been working through various estate and family lawyers for years to get permission to relic-hunt on Thaddeus Farm, one of the few remaining privately owned properties abutting the original Antietam battlefield that had not been pored over by armies of Civil War artifact collectors. The arrangement, done in writing, called for an equal sharing with the current property owners of anything of value that was turned up.

"Hear that?" Larry shouted to Henry.

"Probably a tin can or something," Henry answered.

The buzzer on Larry's metal detector wailed louder than he had ever heard it before. The needle on the gauge smacked hard against the "Full Metal" spot on the far side. And stayed there.

"Hey!" he shouted again to Henry. "Come over and look at this."

They were on the side of a small hill that was sparsely covered with tall grass and short, dark green cedar trees. Years of water runoff had cleared a rough ten-yard-wide grooved path down the side of the hill where Larry and Henry were now standing. They had come down the hill together, with Henry on the right, Larry on the left. Each had the responsibility of passing his detector over every inch of ground on his side of an imaginary line that separated them. Most serious Civil War relic hunters were mindful of the story of Johnny Rinker, a paramedic from Baltimore who had spent four days tracking a recently opened battlefield site south of Fredericksburg, Virginia, and found nothing but a couple of belt buckles. A week later, a fifteen-year-old boy on his first battlefield hunt came in with a Boy Scout troop and discovered a Confederate officer's sword that was considered so rare and special it sold at a New York auction for twelve thousand dollars. Henry had been at a Civil War buffs meeting in Vicksburg, Mississippi, the next spring and heard Johnny Rinker speak the famous words: "It was in a small patch that I somehow missed."

Henry came over to Larry. "Must be a battleship down there," he said after looking at the gauge.

"What should we do?" Larry said.

"Do some digging, that's what."

Each took a small folding shovel out of a pouch that hung on his belt like a holster. The shovels, designed specially for relic hunting, were made of hardened steel and aluminum.

Larry and Henry dropped to their knees and started moving the soft earth away. It was moist and easy to penetrate and move.

Within a few minutes, Larry's tool struck an object. He and Henry used their hands to shove away the dirt.

"Got something," Henry said. "Got something. Got something."

So did Larry.

"I think I've got the piece of a weapon," Henry said.

"I think I've got the piece of a person," Larry said.

"What?"

"Here . . . damn! . . . Look."

What Larry had was a foot-long bone. Henry saw immediately it was human. It was a leg bone. No, an arm bone. Yes, it was an arm bone. The upper arm? Maybe.

Henry took the bone from Larry, turned it over and around and up and down. "It's part of a person, that's for sure," he said.

Larry, using his small shovel and hands, continued to squish through the wet black dirt.

"Look," he said to Henry.

Larry had a handful of small bones. Foot bones? Finger bones?

Henry turned to working through the dirt in front of him. In a few moments he said to Larry, "Here's our metal."

Henry was holding something that despite many years and much rust and deterioration was still recognizable as a pistol—a revolver. A very old revolver.

"What have we got, Henry?" Larry asked.

"Something important, that's what."

"You mean some*body,* don't you?"

"He had a good weapon, that's for sure. This is a Colt."

"I feel like a grave robber."

"You are, but it's for a good cause."

"What cause?" asked Larry.

"Civil War history," Henry replied.

"We don't know if this guy is even from the Civil War. He could have been put here last year or last month, for all we know."

"Wrong, the Colt's Civil War," said Henry. "And look at this."

He held up a piece of metal that was covered in dirt and a white-green patina. "This is an officer's sword-belt plate," he said. "What we have here is somebody who was a Union army officer, that is what we have."

"Well, let's stop right here then," Larry said. He removed his hands from the dirt.

"Stop? What are you talking about?"

"This is a graveyard or something, Henry. Let's cover him back up, get out of here, and leave him be." Larry, thirty pounds heavier and two inches taller than Henry, stood up.

"You're crazy," Henry said. "This is the kind of find I have been dreaming about." Henry moved his hands and arms into another area of fresh earth. In a few moments he came up with another small bone. A piece of a shoulder?

"Let's go call the Park Service then. They can turn this over to their history and archeology people."

"No way. This is private land. I have all of the permissions. We're fully legal. Get down here and help me. We've got something important, we've got something . . ."

Larry moved his left leg and foot right in front of Henry's face and crouched body. "I say stop it. This is a graveyard. We're leaving it for the Park Service."

"This is *not* a graveyard." Henry tried to shove Larry's leg away.

"Don't do that!" Larry leaned down and pushed Henry, who lost his balance and fell backward.

"You big jerk," Henry said, crawling back to a stable position. He swung his shovel around and hit Larry's left shin.

Larry screamed with pain and in a raging reflex raised his shovel high above his head. Henry threw his hands up to protect himself and rolled away. "OK, OK," he said. "We'll do it your way."

"Henry, my God, Henry," said Larry, lowering his shovel. "I almost bashed your head open."

"I know, I know," Henry said.

Both men were literally shaking. Larry reached down and helped pull Henry to his feet. "I'm so sorry," Larry said. And they fell into a rough, quick embrace.

Henry said, "Go call the Park Service."

Kenneth Allbritten was the major force. Roland and I might have waited at least until our second, possibly even our third, year of studies were completed before enlisting in the army. We were both eighteen and students at Yale who had yet to directly address and debate the overriding issues of the war as they affected us personally. Our lives centered on our readings and studies and on our circle of friends and acquaintances and young ladies that made up our environment and attracted our minds in New Haven and East Preston—and occasionally New York or Boston.

But Kenneth Allbritten, the kind of man God had in mind when he created an American nation and people, made us see that our Union's need could not wait for us to become more accomplished scholars in Latin, mathematics, the physical sciences, literature, philosophy, and the other areas of higher learning as well as those connected to the skills necessary to function well in our social environment. He made us understand the Union's need was matched in intensity only by our own to be a part of our nation's destiny.

Kenneth was two years older and thus two years ahead of us in the world and down the road of life. He had already earned his Yale degree, having done so in three years with a skill and drive that marveled those at Yale as well as those of us who admired his accomplishment from home in East Preston. Everyone who spoke of Kenneth Allbritten spoke of him as a young man with a future that would benefit not only himself and those he loved but men and women and children and institutions of all kinds, purposes, and locations.

He was, they said, destined to lead and to achieve, to be believed and to be honored.

Though barely twenty years of age, he was commissioned a lieutenant of Volunteers in the U.S. Army directly from his matriculation and was immediately dispatched for training in the military and leadership skills he would need to command. He returned on horseback to East Preston one radiant Sunday evening in full uniform and regalia as a man with a special recruitment mission given him personally by the governor of Connecticut and other notables. He was one of many officers sent throughout our state to raise the new regiment in the name of Connecticut.

Our house on Maple Avenue, a place that had lovingly spawned and nurtured and sheltered us Randolphs for countless years of joy, was one of his stops. We had been notified in advance of his planned visit, and we welcomed him with pleasure.

The appearance of Lieutenant Kenneth Allbritten was dazzling to any eye. His erect, stout body and a blossomed and trimmed mustache above a set and determined mouth gave him the bearing of a man in charge of himself if not more. His uniform tunic, perfectly cut and worn, was dark blue and trimmed with large shining gold buttons. His trousers were a lighter blue, his black boots were shined as if to be a mirror, his gloves were beige leather and fit for the roughest or the softest of missions, his kepi was a blend of dark blue and gold with a patent-leather black bill.

On his right hip was a .44 Colt revolver that he, when queried, said was given to him by his father, one of our town's most prosperous and dedicated citizens, as a special gift for war.

I had not the power of foresight or nightmare to know then what an instrument of devastation that revolver was to become to so many of our lives.

Don Spaniel always felt slightly apologetic and uncomfortable whenever he put the fingers of his own two hands down into the soil of a place like this. He felt he should speak to the long-dead people, he should explain himself, he should ask their permission to be here—to disturb them. He wanted them to know that he meant no harm and he would do no harm. He wanted them to know that he only wanted to get to know them and to understand who they were and what they did and why.

I am here to tell your story, Union soldier, not to disturb your peace.

It was just before ten o'clock the morning after the discovery of the remains. He had been called last night and had left his Washington town house—technically in the Shirlington area of Arlington, Virginia—shortly after daylight, driving his car as fast as it would carry him.

There was no one else at Thaddeus Farm with him now except two of the armed National Park Service police officers from a detail sent to keep the area secure. They had cordoned it off with yellow plastic tape mounted on wooden stakes and placed a large canvas tarpaulin over the grave itself and the items the hunters had uncovered. The Antietam National Battlefield superintendent had arranged with the farm's owners for the Park Service to take control of the site for excavation and analysis. A final determination on what might happen to the remains and artifacts would be made later.

Don was pleased to consider the possibility that it could mean eventually dealing again with Faye Lee Sutton, a lawyer in the Interior Department counsel's office. He had promised to call her for an evening of a movie or a meal last year—or was it the year before?—but he had never gotten around to it. They had worked, and flirted, together while resolving the ownership of a remarkably well-preserved Confederate soldier's diary found on Park Service land near Richmond. The soldier's heirs said it should go to them, but Faye Lee Sutton had successfully argued that historical artifacts found on federal land were the property of the government.

Romance with Faye Lee Sutton was something to think about later. There was archeology to do first.

Don was wearing faded blue jeans, a heavy dark green workshirt, and thick-soled, waterproof walking boots, as well as his fedora. Reg Womach, his Smithsonian friend, wasn't the only one who called him "Indiana" or "Harrison." They were certainly better nicknames than one Don had for a while in high school. A guy in sophomore English class started calling Don "Icky"—for Ichabod Crane, the schoolmaster described by Washington Irving in "The Legend of Sleepy Hollow" as being easily mistaken for "a scarecrow eloped from a cornfield." "Icky" stuck until Don, risen to his full six-foot-four height, made the starting basketball team his junior year. Then he became known as "The Knife," for his ability to coolly cut his way through a tight zone defense for a layup.

Don's mission this morning was to make an overview inspection of the site that included taking a look at the remains and artifacts that were visible. The full dig would be done in a few days by a team of archeologists and archeology students he would assemble as quickly as possible.

The first thing he did after removing the tarp was to make a record of what he saw upon arrival, using a thirty-five-millimeter camera and a small tape recorder. He photographed and noted the several small piles of dirt, the imprints of the two relic hunters' shovels and boots and knees, and, most important, the bones and artifacts they had extracted before they stopped digging.

Don, unlike some of his anal archeologist and Park Service colleagues, considered himself to be on the same side as most Civil War enthusiasts, including even the reenactors, those intense souls, some of whom actually began to believe they really were Civil War soldiers. But Don's special affection was for the relic hunters, the thousands of obsessed amateurs who spent their weekends scouring Civil War sites with their instincts and metal detectors. They were, to Don's view, as much a part of the crew dedicated to the discovery, study, and preservation of the realities, legends, and lessons of the Civil War as he was. Yes, there were some crazies bent on restoring the Confederacy and/or slavery, and there were some hunter-collectors who sometimes dug for relics illegally or inappropriately. But those renegades were the exceptions.

And, as he surveyed what lay before him now, he was particularly thankful that two men from Sharpsburg, whatever their motivations, had brought their detectors and their passions to this particular piece of ground.

Into the tape recorder, Don said, "A pistol . . . rusted but not in bad shape . . . looks like a .44 Colt. . . . That means he probably bought it himself. . . . A sword-belt plate . . . definitely an officer's . . . buttons . . . also officer . . . no ID disk.

"Bones . . . the largest . . . upper arm . . . looks like the right humerus . . . four smaller ones . . . fingers."

Then, down on his knees, using the brush and a small stainless-steel trowel, he made a few careful turns of the dirt. Several buttons and what looked like the sole of a boot turned up. Then came a few scraps of cloth. From the soldier's uniform, he figured—and said so into his recorder. The same for a small metal buckle that appeared to be from a piece of a soldier's personal equipment—a pack, valise, or some such.

Don continued to move the dirt away until he had before him the outline, still thinly covered, of what looked to be the bones of a complete human skeleton.

"Let me introduce myself, Union soldier—if that's in fact what you are," he said. "My name is Donald Jackson Spaniel. I will know for sure what you are, and I will know your full name before I rest. That's a promise, sir."

Don had always been routinely emotional about his work, a fact that had scared away more than one potential wife and/or steady girlfriend. But not even one of them, assuming any were even interested, could deny that what lay before him was truly worth getting worked up about. Faye Lee Sutton, at least, would certainly get it—he was fairly sure.

Archeologists and anthropologists seldom had a full skeleton to examine from any Civil War battle. That was particularly true at Antietam, which was the single bloodiest day in the history of American warfare. More than twenty-three thousand men were killed or wounded that September 17, 1862. And when the fighting was over, a thirty-three-square-mile area was littered with bodies, in some places stacked one on another. There was not time, people, or resources to give them all a proper burial right then so both the Union and Confederate armies asked local townspeople and farmers to bury what dead were on their properties. The citizens had little choice. The smell of those decaying bodies and the hygiene problems they created were intolerable for the people around Sharpsburg. But three years later, the state of Maryland decided to create a cemetery for the Union dead of Antietam at the northern end of Sharpsburg. Similar places for Confederate bodies were set aside in Hagerstown, up the road, and in nearby Shepherdstown, West Virginia. People were offered a two-dollar-per-body fee for digging up a body and turning it in for burial in the new cemeteries. Unfortunately, all the holder of a body had to have to qualify for the fee was a head and one or two long bones, plus an ID disk the soldiers wore around their necks or one of the hundreds of small wood headboards that were used to mark graves and identify who was buried there. In most cases, the rest of the dead soldier's remains, including usually the rib cage, was covered back over and again forgotten. It was the discovery of those partial remains many years later that most often ended up being a concern—and a frustration— for Don. There was often not enough to go on for him and forensic anthropologists like Reg Womach to draw definite identifications or other conclusions.

The Civil War was pretty much Don Spaniel's full-time job. Most of his work as an archeologist for the Park Service involved filtering through and deciphering the mysteries and stories in the ground in Virginia and Maryland where the men of the North and South did so much violence to one another. Interest in the war came to him naturally. He had grown up in Harrisonburg, Virginia, where his father had taught American history at James

Madison University and his mother had been active in various historical-preservation efforts.

Don traced the roots of his interest in Civil War archeology specifically to a sixth-grade field trip to the nearby New Market battlefield, where he saw people on their hands and knees sifting dirt at a spot where several hundred young Virginia Military Institute cadets had charged the Union's line. One of the archeologists told Don and his classmates that he could not imagine any work more exciting or rewarding than "searching the ground in the present for clues to what had happened there in the past."

Twenty-five years later, here Don was using a small whisk broom to remove some loose dirt to better see a long bone. He said into the tape recorder: "Something from a leg? Yes. The left femur—the bone that goes from the hip to the knee. Looks like that of a male."

He skimmed away some more earth. "Here's the left patella—the kneecap . . . and . . . yes . . . below that a tibia and a fibula." And then an ankle and some toes—tarsals, metatarsals, and phalanges.

Hear that, Reg? Too bad you're not here to see what I *know about bones.* He couldn't help but throw a few imagined lines to Reg Womach, the real expert, who within a few days would have these bones delivered to him in plastic bags. Spaniel could imagine the delight his Smithsonian friend would share in having so many from one Antietam soldier to examine. There was no telling what Reg would learn about this man—this man who presumably died on this ground more than 130 years ago.

There was also no telling what he, the archeologist, might be able to determine from the study of that pistol and buckle and shoe and the buttons and anything else found with the dead soldier's remains.

But Don knew he was going to need more than Reg Womach's enthusiasm and expertise and his own hard work. Don knew the basics and the overall significance and context of what happened here on the banks of the Antietam on that September day in 1862, but he did not really know the detail and grit of the battle itself and, most particularly, of the fight for Burnside Bridge. Fortunately, he knew where to turn for that knowledge.

To another man who lived emotionally in the past, Gary Wayne Doleman: colonel, U.S. Army, retired; professor of history, Shepherd College, retired; world's number one expert, battle of Antietam, active.

But first things first.

Don, still on his knees, leaned farther forward for a closer look, carefully brushing away thin layers of dirt, but only enough to see and confirm as he moved his intense gaze up the body that the skeleton had the full complement of bones.

He arrived at the skull. To a forensic anthropologist like Reg the skull was a road map, a personal history book unlike any other. With the skull, particularly one with some teeth, there were few identification miracles that were not possible.

Don could see the outlines of the skull there under the dirt. He whisked away another tiny bit of dirt. He expected to see the signs of the cavities where the eyes and the nose had been and the mouth and possibly a few teeth. But it was the *back* of the head he was looking at. At the base of the skull, he saw a hole the size of a large coin.

Don picked up the tape recorder again. "It would appear the subject was shot through the head."

Wait a minute. Something, as they say, was wrong with this picture. He suddenly realized that he had not noticed the most obvious characteristic about these remains. This man had been buried *facedown*!

He whispered into the recorder, "This is most unusual. Most people are buried on their backs."

He set the recorder down and looked hard at the skull again. "Why did somebody bury you this way, Mr. Union soldier?" he asked aloud in a conversational tone.

Don felt a twitching in his shoulders, a tingling in his chest, some heat in his face. He took off his fedora and laid it on the ground beside him.

If confronted at that moment, Don might not have denied a suggestion that he truly expected an answer from the dead Union soldier.

Kenneth Allbritten spoke to me and to my parents and sister, who sat with me in our south parlor, a room I always held dear for its fragrance, which was a mixture of lavender and rose and book bindings. Kenneth said: "I am here to assemble a company of men that will fight as one, as no others have ever done. The future of everything we as Americans and sons of Connecticut believe in is at risk. If we fail to answer the call to muster, then we not only fail in our duty, we may ultimately fail in our very existence.

"The Rebs are on the run from the superior force and spirit and rightness of the Union army. Those of us who wish to participate in the ultimate test of our manhood and patriotism must do so now or forever thereafter be damned to explain to our brethren and our sons to come as well as to ourselves and God why we were not there, why we did not hear the summons of our time, our generation. The tests of our mettle that come to us in a lifetime are few.

"I will be at the recruitment tent on the square at eight o'clock in the morning, Albert. Come packed sparely and prepared bravely to do your duty for your country and your Connecticut. I offer you one hundred dollars as an enlistment bonus plus a forty-five-dollar uniform allowance and pay of thirteen dollars a month to sign up for three years."

I told him that I would be there in the morning to accept the offer and the challenge of my state and nation.

My mother and sister cried; my father smiled with pride. I had been on a sure course since birth that would lead to my going into business with my father, the most illustrious and prosperous merchant of clothing, jewelry, and other personal items in our community. "There is time to wait for 'Randolph & Son,'" he said, "but there is no time to wait for preserving our Union."

Kenneth Allbritten also went that evening to Elmwood, the Mackenzie home, which was considerably larger in size and elegance than our substantial but humbler house five easy blocks eastward. Roland's father was one of the few and most distinguished attorneys in East Preston, one of the other few and most distinguished being Kenneth Allbritten's father. Both Roland and Kenneth were namesakes and treasured sons, as was I.

Roland, distraught and disheveled from anxiety and anguish, came to our house at a late hour that same night with a plea to me that challenged the promise I had made to Kenneth a few hours before:

"My father says the Union army is poorly equipped, poorly supported, and poorly led. He says the Rebs are not yet on the run. He says it is Lincoln who is doing the running through a sad list of his generals, most of them incompetent and arrogant, in a frantic effort to find someone to mount a proper fight against the Rebels. He says to join the Union army now is to join an exercise in immediate futility and possibly even humiliation if not certain

death. He says the Rebs, other than Lee, are ignorant illiterate simpletons who will eventually be brought to heel by their own bumbling incompetence, and there will come a time to be a part of the effort to conquer and vanquish them. But until then, there are others of our age and persuasion and position in Connecticut and elsewhere to handle the situation and the obligations. He says I should wait until I have my Yale degree so that I can be commissioned and until the Union is in a better position to fight and to triumph. He says if I will wait he will follow the example of Kenneth's father in providing me ample funds for the most elegant uniforms and personal firearms befitting my position as an officer in the United States Army. He says there are times in life for action and immediacy and times when caution and delay are demanded. The latter is the situation at this moment, he says."

His father's argument was a telling and persuasive one, but I had to let it flow through me to no consequence.

"I gave Kenneth my word that I would be at the tent at eight o'clock in the morning," I said to Roland.

"I did as well," Roland said.

"Then your father's arguments, no matter their worth and weight, cannot prevail."

Roland, his anguish now only a memory, agreed, and we rode away to Hartford together the next morning with seven other young men of East Preston to our mixed destinies with the Eleventh Connecticut Volunteer Regiment.

3

Colonel Gary Wayne Doleman, eighty-one, and Don Spaniel, thirty-seven, two tall men of the past, stood together on the high ground in front of the Union soldier's remains.

The colonel was, as always, dressed in starched camouflage army fatigues and combat boots. He wore his thick light gray hair in the crew-cut style they gave him when he enlisted in the U.S. Army at the age of twenty-eight. Despite a weakening heart, his six-foot-three trim body showed the erectness and exercise remnants of a man who cared about bearing, impression—and command.

" 'May he rest in peace' is the proper and appropriate thing to say, I believe," said the colonel, looking down at the bones and artifacts of the Union soldier where Spaniel had left them the afternoon before, still under the protection of park police. "But there is no rest for him, is there, Doctor Spaniel?"

Clearly not wanting or expecting an answer, the colonel then turned from the Thaddeus Farm hillside grave and looked west and below to the scene of war.

"Battles such as the one fought on this ground are never really over. The force of the collision and the rawness of the death and the loudness of the screams preclude certain rest. We will always be called upon from time to time to deal with the remains from what happened here."

Dramatic lectures from the colonel were always part of the bargain. You could pick his brain and his wisdom, but you got the proceeds spoken in his deep, booming voice with the pentameters of a poet, the flourishes of an actor.

"Look over there, young Doctor Spaniel. From here it seems so peaceful, so serene."

Don certainly agreed with that. There were only a handful of visitors in the distance walking around the running creek, dirt paths, small monuments, wooden fences, thick green grass, and bushes. There was no noise except for that of rustling leaves and of a few lonesome birds. It was hard to imagine anything awful or violent ever happening here.

"There is that damnable bridge, just two hundred yards away," said the colonel. "That bridge of death and suffering that caused so many people to make so many stupid decisions, so many men to react so heroically to those decisions, so many men to die because of the decisions and the reactions. Seldom have so many died because of the stupidity and heroism of so few. Stupidity and heroism are a deadly combination, Doctor Spaniel."

This old man simply could not resist lavishing context and philosophy with his dramatic lessons and specifics. He had been an American history professor at the University of Michigan when he enlisted during World War Two. After officers-training school and being wounded as a tank commander in Patton's Third Army in Europe, he was assigned to the army's history section. He then joined the faculty at the Army War College at Carlisle, Pennsylvania, until he left the army to join the history department at Shepherd College in Shepherdstown, West Virginia, twenty years ago. Spaniel knew that it was while he was at Carlisle, only eighty miles north of Sharpsburg, that Colonel Doleman's obsession with the battle of Antietam had taken hold. He once told Don it was his astonishment at the unparalleled willingness of so many good young men to die in such an honorable way that locked his mind into wanting to know everything. And now there really was no living person who knew more about what happened here—right here—on September 17, 1862.

"Listen, doctor, listen. Do you hear the awful noise? Do you hear the incredible roar of cannon and rifle fire? Do you hear the whack of shells against trees? Do you hear it? The cracking of bones. Do you hear that? Do you hear the screaming?"

Yes, Don Spaniel thought he heard it.

Then Colonel Doleman said, "Let's move down toward that damnable bridge over the Antietam. Antietam. Not everyone pronounces it correctly. *Ann-tee-tum,* with a slight pause after the *Ann* and a slight accent on the *tee*. Ann . . . *tee*tum. Antietam. The creek, the battle—the bloodiest day."

The bloodiest day. Don knew the basics. It was September 1862. Robert E. Lee had just scored a major victory in the second battle of Bull Run. He wanted to capitalize on it quickly in hopes of coaxing Britain and France into officially recognizing the Confederacy and thus dramatically turn the tide of the war. A major thrust into the North would be perfect, he decided. Maryland, just across the Potomac, was chosen, most particularly with the hope that the British and the French, as well as all others, would see the people of Maryland rise up in support of Confederate troops. Through mysterious circumstances, a copy of Lee's marching order fell into Union hands, and Lee's outnumbered Army of Northern Virginia, originally divided into two pincerlike forces, was pursued by the Union's Army of the Potomac. Lee fell back to a small stretch of Maryland land between Antietam Creek and the Potomac, where he decided to make a stand. The only things that kept him from being completely destroyed were his own military smarts and a series of mistakes by the cautious Union general on the other side, George B. McClellan. But the end result of Antietam was seen as enough of a Union victory to provide political cover for President Abraham Lincoln to issue the Emancipation Proclamation.

Don and the colonel began walking down the hillside through thick grass and bushes and small trees.

"Can you smell the stench, Doctor Spaniel, as we get closer? The smoke from the firing of those weapons? It's in the eyes, and it's in the nose and the ears. Do you smell blood? Do you smell the feces and the urine—the most pungent of the battlefield smells? It all pours out of a dying body. Everything pours out with the life. And it stinks to the highest of the heavens."

Don Spaniel could smell it all.

He had found Colonel Doleman, this most remarkable man, yesterday—via telephone—in the Shepherd College library in Shepherdstown, an eighteenth-century West Virginia village just over the Potomac and five miles down the road from Sharpsburg. It was where Lee's forces forded the Potomac and slipped back into Virginia the days immediately after the battle of Antietam.

Over the phone, the colonel had said the dead soldier could have come from one of the New York outfits, probably the Fifty-first, or possibly the Forty-eighth or Fifty-first Pennsylvania. This morning, after seeing the exact location of the burial site, he decided the man was more likely from one of the three Connecticut regiments involved in the battle for Burnside Bridge.

"If forced to state my opinion at this moment," he said now as they walked, "I would say he was a member of the Eleventh Connecticut."

In a world of his own, the colonel began to set the scene of battle: "There had been a steady rain the night before, but only a drizzle and some fog remained at sunrise on the seventeenth. The temperature was in the mid-sixties, and then the sun came out and it went into the seventies and eighties before the day was done. The humidity was a bit higher than normal, but otherwise it was a perfect September day, a perfect day for killing people."

They had walked less than fifty yards to a blacktop road that separated Thaddeus Farm from the official grounds of the Antietam Battlefield.

Colonel Doleman was breathing heavily. He needed to stop walking for a few moments, but he did not stop talking.

"We're all killers, Doctor Spaniel," he said, pausing against a small sycamore tree. "That's why wars work. Properly engaged or enraged, any one of us and every one of us can kill a fellow human being or commit an absolutely horrid act of brutality against him. All of the tactics and the strategies and the bullets and the shells and the bombs and the bayonets and the medals and the uniforms and the flags and the songs are weapons of killing, weapons to administer and justify killing or to avoid and curse killing."

Don agreed with the colonel but made no response.

"Why is it that old people send their young off to die and then are surprised and upset when they do?" asked the colonel, looking down and away at the bridge rather than at Don. The colonel's questions were most always rhetorical.

They walked across the road. The bridge, now barely 125 yards away, was there before and below them—getting easier to see, to comprehend as the silent symbol of the bloodletting that happened on and around it 134 years ago.

The colonel continued his self-absorbed narrative: "The first try at taking the bridge was at about nine o'clock in the morning. McClellan—oh, what a fool he was—sent the order to General

Ambrose Burnside—oh, what a fool *he* was. This, right here where we're walking and looking, was the left flank of the attack against the Confederates' right flank. There were to be three parts of the Union assault: one on the far right, one in the middle, and this one on the left. They were supposed to be coordinated. Right and left at the same time, forcing Lee, who may have been foolish at times—particularly later at Gettysburg—but was not a fool, to reinforce both ways, thus clearing the way for the main Union force to charge easily down the center into Sharpsburg. It happened correctly on the right but not over here. This bridge crossing was expected to be easy and quick. There were ten thousand men in the Ninth Corps on this side under the command of Burnside and only a few hundred on the other commanded by a Confederate politician-turned-general named Toombs. Easy and quick was the word, the expectation."

The colonel took a long breath. Don thought for a moment Doleman was in need of another tree to lean on. But that wasn't the problem. It was the story he was now to tell that required an extra breath.

"At 0900, some kids from the Eleventh Connecticut were sent down from this high ground—this *very* high ground we're now standing on—to secure the entrance to the bridge from the left side, this side. An Ohio brigade was to come to the bridge from there, from the right side, from over that hill and those trees over there about four hundred yards. The Ohios and the Connecticuts were to meet there at the mouth of the bridge and storm across. That was the plan. Easy and quick.

"But the Ohio brigade got lost or confused. Whatever the cause, doctor, they came out way, way over there, some three hundred fifty yards beyond the bridge and out of the action. That left the boys from the Eleventh Connecticut, who did as they were told and led, to be the ones to die. They were sitting ducks. Sitting ducks in a way that bordered on the criminal, if you must know, sir."

Don had heard that term *criminal* used to describe the situation of the Union soldiers involved in the battle for Burnside Bridge. But he had not, until now, focused on exactly what that meant.

With his left hand, the colonel pointed across the creek, up into some trees on a high bank. "Look over there to the Confederate side and you will see why. There were some four hundred Confederate riflemen over there. Most of them were from the Twentieth Georgia. They commanded the high ground in the way that a boy at the carnival commands the view at a shooting gallery. Those Georgia boys were shooting from well-hidden and protected positions in trees and trenches. They looked down there at these poor Connecticut boys running across that open field toward the bridge and simply mowed them down one at a time. Those shooting Georgia boys in gray wasted very few shots. Most every little rocket of hot lead hit some part of some running Connecticut boy in blue."

And Don Spaniel had no trouble imagining a piece of hot lead piercing the stomach or head or leg of a running Connecticut boy in a blue uniform.

"Let's keep moving, doctor," said the colonel. "The terrifying awfulness of what happened will become so obvious to you, so terribly obvious. I have approached that bridge many times, hundreds of times. But the terrible awfulness of what it meant for those kids always strikes me. Always. And I hereby pray that it always will for me."

The colonel turned them up a two-foot-wide dirt path, up a small rise toward a clump of tall trees.

"This way are the two Eleventh Connecticut markers. They're off the beaten route of the regular tourists—but let's take a look, sir. Their story is there."

It took several minutes for the slow-moving retired army colonel and his archeologist companion to mount the incline and enter a shaded area enclosed on all sides and above by trees. A gray monument and a blue metal tablet were in the open space in the center, which was about ten yards in diameter.

The colonel and Don walked first to the inch-thick, yard-square tablet that sat three feet off the ground on a pedestal. In raised white letters was written the official story.

"I will read it. I will read it out loud," said the colonel.

Although Spaniel felt perfectly able to grasp the words and their full meaning all by himself silently, he said that would be fine, sir.

The colonel spoke as if addressing a crowd of hundreds.

" 'Eleventh Connecticut Infantry, Colonel Henry W. Kingsbury, Commanding . . .

" 'September seventeenth, eighteen-sixty-two . . .

" 'This regiment opened the engagement on this part of the field on the morning of September seventeenth. It was partially deployed in skirmishing order and preceded Crook's Brigade, Kanawha Division, in an attack on the Stone Bridge. It descended the hill on the east and passed over this ground under a severe fire of Confederate artillery on the high ground west and infantry concealed in the woods, in pits and behind stone fences, loose rocks, and rails, commanding the bridge and its approaches. The left and center reached the banks of the stream, the right the level ground between this and the bridge. Colonel Kingsbury was mortally wounded a few feet northwest of this spot. Captain John Griswold was killed in the stream opposite the end of the Rohrbaugh Lane. Lieutenant Kenneth Allbritten died in a ravine two hundred feet north of here. And after a severe contest in which the regiment suffered a loss of one hundred and thirty-nine killed and wounded, it retired to the shelter of the wooded ravine running north past this spur.'

"So much said with so few words."

"Amen," said Don with one word.

"Behind you there is that wooded ravine," said the colonel. "It was back up in there that the young Lieutenant Allbritten was killed. Death had just jumped him into a higher position of command after Kingsbury and Griswold fell. Then a rebel cannon shot hit Allbritten right square in the face. Tore his face and all of his head away. He was only a kid. Most of them were kids in age but not in courage and guts. They were men."

Don knew all of that from his own studies of the Civil War, but his particular thoughts now were about that Union officer—if that, in fact, was what he was—whose remains lay back on that Thaddeus Farm hillside. How old was he? Was he a kid in age, a man in courage and guts? What did his voice sound like? Was it high-pitched or a deep baritone? Was he articulate? Did anybody love him?

"Right where you are standing, doctor, is where Colonel Kingsbury took the last shot that killed him. He was shot four times. First in the foot, down near the stream, and then in the leg as he was moving up this way, and then finally here in the shoulder and abdomen. He hung on for a day and died at a farm back up over this hill. Exactly there where you are is where he was standing when a shot from one of the Georgia boys hit him."

Don moved a long, quick step to his right.

"There's nothing still there, of course," said the colonel with a smile. "But I admire your respect reflexes."

Thank you, colonel.

"Kingsbury was only twenty-five years old, but he was no boy, no kid. He had blond hair, a mustache, blue eyes. It's hard to imagine a man who died one hundred thirty-four years ago right where you're standing with blond hair, a mustache, and blue eyes, isn't it?"

Don nodded. But the nod was a small lie. Don had no difficulty imagining a blond man with blue eyes and a mustache dying right here. The setting and the colonel's dramatic words helped, but Don Spaniel was already pretty good at imagining such events. That's mostly what he did for a living.

The colonel moved to the six-foot-tall granite and marble monument to the Eleventh. At a glance it resembled a tombstone for somebody important—possibly the town banker or county judge—except this one had a yard-wide, eighteen-inch-high rectangular bronze diorama of the battle for the bridge that included a man, clearly Griswold, in the creek waving a sword high above his head. On the other side of the monument were the names of the dead.

"Colonel Kingsbury's there on the top of the list. Do you see that?"

Yes, I see that, Don thought but did not say.

"Griswold is second. Then the others. Thirty-eight others. Including Allbritten. These are just the ones in the Eleventh who died on this side of the bridge."

The colonel suddenly stopped talking and moved away, back down the path into the open field toward the Antietam. Don followed and then joined him by his right side.

And soon the colonel resumed.

"It was open here in this field that day, mostly as it is now. There was a wooden-rail fence here that resembled this one."

The fence was waist high, made of crossed timbers.

"The Connecticut boys and others afterward came down this

way and headed for the creek bank. They were taking fire every step of the way. Artillery from over behind that high ground. But it was the small-arms fire that was so deadly. Look over there at the Georgia infantry positions. Barely seventy-five yards from there down to here. They must have thought they were the ones who had died and gone to heaven. None of them could ever have dreamed that killing Yanks would be made this easy; none of them could ever have dreamed that the generals on the other side would be so stupid."

And then, almost as if it came out of nowhere, there was the running water of the Antietam.

The colonel's words paralleled Don's own private reaction. "Look at that water. Beautiful, isn't it? Clear as fine glass."

Don Spaniel would have added only that it reminded him of a stream outside Harrisonburg in which he sometimes fished with his father.

"Only fifty feet across. Not very deep either. Barely chest high on most men. Burnside's whole corps of ten thousand men could have waded across in a few minutes or so. The Georgians would have had no choice but to move out of here. But Burnside sent no scouts out ahead of time to check the depth and the fordability of the creek. He just assumed the only way across this little puddle of water was over that little, narrow bridge."

The colonel stopped and said, "It was about here that Captain Griswold decided to try it on his own. A few of his men—not more than a half dozen—were with him when he jumped into the water and headed for the other side. The Georgians took a bead on them. All but the captain turned back to this side. The captain kept moving. About midstream, he took a bullet that tore open his chest. He still didn't stop. Another hit him in the neck. Still moving, he got to the bank on the other side. See where I'm pointing? Right there. It seems so close. He got there, climbed up on the bank, and bled to death. We'll go over there in a minute. I consider it hallowed ground."

Hallowed ground. In the literature of the Civil War, it was a term commonly used to describe the ground of battle—*any* ground of battle. Don Spaniel, whose life's work was dealing with what lay in that ground, shared the reverence that went with the two words.

The colonel was now talking about Captain Griswold. "A Yale graduate, he was what they called a cultured man of the liberal arts. The men who served with him before Antietam said he delighted in talking about Horace and Victor Hugo and Saint Augustine as he marched. Imagine that in the U.S. Army of today. He was also twenty-five when he died. Aren't you glad some fool general didn't send you off to die when you were twenty-five?"

Don, if answers from him had been part of this dialogue, would have replied: "Yes and no, colonel." Don had come of military-service age after the Vietnam war and the end of the draft, a fact that gave him and his parents a terrific sense of relief at the time. But increasingly since, Don longed for military experience. The deeper his work and mind forced him into the world of battle and combat and killing, the more he wished he had a personal frame of reference for it all. His longings and wishes had led him to believe that there should be mandatory national service, that all young people, male and female, should be required to spend two years or so in the military or some comparable government service. Most people, particularly women, he mentioned it to thought that was an awful idea, but he loved debating it with one and all.

But the colonel wouldn't be interested in such a discussion right now. It was on to the bridge!

"Nothing too impressive to look at, is it, Doctor Spaniel? As a bridge, not much to have caused so much commotion, so much concern, so much death. Barely sixty feet across, less than ten yards wide. Half-circled supports, three of them. Simple stone construction. Shelby Foote described it as a 'narrow, triple-arched stone span' over a 'little copper-colored stream.' It could be a bridge over any quiet little country stream, couldn't it? Let's go across, all right?"

Don had often walked over this little bridge but never before with the colonel, never before accompanied by spoken words that made it so dramatically alive.

"On that morning, where we are putting our feet now, there were bodies and blood. In the final assault at one o'clock by men of Ferrero's Brigade—the Fifty-first New York and the Fifty-first Pennsylvania—they had to run over their own fallen men. Some slipped and fell on the blood. Somebody said it was like running across a dance floor covered with bright red oil. A dance floor covered with bright red oil. A bridge covered with blood. What's the difference between red blood and red oil? Both of them make you fall down. Imagine it, if you will. Imagine being eighteen years old, running under fire four abreast across this bridge, slipping and sliding as you ran on what you knew was the blood of other eighteen-year-olds who had come before you. Imagine it, if you will. . . ."

Don felt his right foot slip. Impossible! He was wearing rubber-sole walking boots, and the bridge's surface was light pea gravel. But now he felt his left foot slip. And he smelled blood—and oil.

In a few moments, they were at the other side—the Confederate side—of the bridge. Don suddenly wished for a break, some quiet, some relief from the relentlessness of the story of this bridge, the vivid images of red, oil, blood, slipping and sliding.

But Colonel Doleman, even with his bad heart and slow legs, was still moving mouth and mind.

"Now look back at the bridge and across, Doctor Spaniel. Go with your imagination to what happened next. Once the bridge was finally secured and the Georgians withdrew from these ridges, Burnside sent his entire force across. More than ten thousand men and about twenty cannons and support supplies rumbled across that narrow little bridge for nearly two hours."

Don's most vivid imagination was spent—used up at the moment. He could not see wagons and horses and cannons and men in blue with rifles and swords squeezing through and over the small structure.

The colonel was still going strong. He turned back toward the Confederate high ground and moved his storytelling toward the conclusion—the end of the bloodiest day.

"They formed an attack line of troops a mile across, facing Sharpsburg over in that direction—south and west," he said, pointing off toward the right. "That's where what remained of Lee's army was braced for a final attack, an attack that if it had come earlier and swifter could have resulted in the complete annihilation of the Confederate army and, most probably, the end of the war.

"But by the time Burnside was ready, a Confederate general named A. P. Hill, who wore a nonregulation red shirt in the field, came up in a forced march from Harpers Ferry. He marched his troops seventeen miles in seven hours, arriving in a cloud of dust just in time to attack the Union's far-left flank and throw most everyone into a state of confusion."

Don followed the colonel up some steps that had been built for Burnside Bridge tourists to go to a parking lot. The colonel climbed very slowly, making each step with both feet before moving on. There were a few times in the full ten minutes it took to make it to the top that Don thought the older man might falter, might drop. But no. Colonel Gary Wayne Doleman was not about to leave his mission unaccomplished.

At the top, it was possible to see the road off in the distance from which General Hill and his troops had come. Don, ready now for his own tour to be over, aroused his imagination one last time.

He saw the troops and a red shirt and the dust.

"One of the worst stories had to do with another Connecticut outfit, the Sixteenth," said the colonel.

Please, thought Spaniel, *no more stories*.

"Kids right out of college, smart kids, but they had been in uniform and under arms only three weeks and had no training in firing or formations or tactics—or survival. They were on the far left in a cornfield when A. P. Hill struck, and they panicked. I mean, they threw down their arms and ran. Not all of them. But many. Who could blame them? Did you know about the Sixteenth, Doctor Spaniel?"

The colonel was looking right at Spaniel, which meant a rare answer was expected this time. Don merely shook his head. And he could feel one last speech coming on.

"Do not think of those boys of the Sixteenth as being dishonorable—of being cowards."

"I don't, colonel. I don't."

"There were no cowards in the fight for this bridge, no men from either side who dishonored themselves. It is important to remember that, Doctor Spaniel, as you go about your business of identifying that man back up there on that hillside."

Don said he would definitely keep that in mind.

And the colonel swept his body back around to face the bridge and get a panoramic view from this high ground of the complete battlefield around it. The cluster of trees in which the Eleventh

Connecticut tablet and memorial stood were visible. So was the wooden fence and, of course, the flowing water of the Antietam and, even way across, up there above the trees and across the road, the Thaddeus Farm hillside.

And here now came the speech.

"What did it all matter? The incompetence of the Union generals prevented their overwhelming force from defeating Lee here at Antietam. McClellan didn't use his reserves, and he didn't even have sense to launch a final killing attack the next day, on the eighteenth. So Lee quietly took his army back across the Potomac to regroup to fight another day. The war lasted another three years, and hundreds of thousands more died before it ended. It could have ended here. It really could have. This battle, this catastrophe here at Antietam was the real Civil War. People pay much attention to Gettysburg and Shiloh and some of the others. This is the place to understand the war.

"This is the place to be astonished that all of these young men, on both sides, so willingly gave their lives. Some of the Confederates believed they had a cause. They must have. But what of these boys from Connecticut and Pennsylvania and Vermont and New York and Minnesota? Most of them had never laid eyes on a black person, so slavery wasn't a real issue to them. What did they care about all of that preserving-the-Union talk from Abraham Lincoln and the other politicians? It is a wonder— an astonishment—there was not more running the other way, that honor so ruled this battlefield."

Don Spaniel suddenly was no longer spent. He felt a welling up of deep sadness but also of an even deeper pride in and identification with what had happened here—on this hallowed ground.

"That is the great mystery of this place and all other places of this war," said the colonel. "Look back over there at that high ground where we began, doctor. What must have this now peace-ful place looked like to most of those young men from over there? It must have looked like death, possibly certain death. And yet they came, time after time after time after time they came across that ground down there toward that damnable bridge.

"I am amazed by it all, young Doctor Spaniel. I will remain amazed by it for however brief a time I have left on this earth.

"Therefore and forever more, I plan to never be far from *this* earth."

Young Doctor Spaniel joined in the colonel's amazement.

I do not wish to delay the telling of our tragedy at the Antietam bridge, but I think some more must be known before proceeding. No, no, that may not be the full and frank truth! Maybe I do wish to delay and delay and delay. Could I harbor a hope that the longer I tarry on the way to that place of hell with this pen in my hand, the lesser the pain the arrival and thus the reliving will send radiating through my body and soul?

Whatever the possible many purposes, there is information that should be known.

We, the Eleventh Connecticut, were a force of 927 officers and men when officially organized and mustered into the U.S. Army at an open field of tents in Hartford on October 24, 1861. We were given uniforms, much less elegant and wear-worthy than Kenneth Allbritten's. Instead of Colt revolvers, we were issued long muskets, with which we did some light marching, firing, and other training. We were told to expect fierce resistance from the Confederate soldiers, who, though mostly ignorant and misguided in their motivation and purpose, believed and fought strongly for their despicable and lost cause.

It is relevant to subsequent events and I hope does not appear boastful for me to report that I prospered as a soldier recruit. I found that I was quick to learn the military tasks and that I was successful in performing them and then patient and direct in instructing others in how to do so. These positives in my performance, I cannot hide my pride in saying, came to the notice and pleasure of Kenneth Allbritten and the other officers in our company and brigade. Within a short matter of a very few weeks, I was promoted from private to sergeant and given responsibilities commensurate with my rank.

There is no doubt or question that being made a sergeant made my head and chest expand, my back stiffen, my pace smarten, my purpose heighten. I mean no disrespect or disregard when I say that my good fortune was not greeted as praiseworthy by Roland Mackenzie. He, too, drew a promotion, but it came at a slower pace and was to corporal, immediately below sergeant, which had the effect of my being superior to him in rank and responsibility. I made a serious and frequent effort to persuade my close and cherished friend that the choice between us was a military formality and meant nothing of consequence. He did not accept my explanation. What he failed to appreciate was that his attitude, understandable as it surely was in basic terms of the human experience and personality, tended to deprecate my own achievement.

The relevant observation is that when we left Hartford for war, I had the iron impression that Roland might never forgive or forget what Kenneth Allbritten had done to him.

Roland referred to the event in heavy voice and tone as "the slight."

4

Don put out calls to the University of Maryland and George Washington University for help. Anybody interested in a little volunteer digging work? No pay but a lot of great experience in the real world of archeology? He had used faculty and students from both schools to great advantage before because the more people out there on their hands and knees sifting through dirt or whatever, the greater the odds of finding things that mattered. Not even in his dreamworld would he ever have enough full-time archeologists and assistants on his staff to do a full dig under any kind of efficient or realistic deadline.

Eight outsiders showed up for the dig. They and five personnel from the Park Service first spent three days marking off, mapping, photographing, and carefully working the ground with metal detectors. They put red plastic survey flags in the seven spots over an acre-and-a-half area around the grave where they had picked up signs—no matter how slight—of something metallic down below. But the follow-up digging turned up nothing more than a few tiny bones and some buttons, as well as hunks of metal from modern-day farming tools. The conclusion by the end of the third day was that there was no burial ground, no battlefield graveyard here. The pros hadn't turned up anything more than the amateur relic hunters had. There was one man, alone.

There was absolutely nothing in what they found that shed any new light or information on the life or times of that man. His bones, wrapped in plastic bubble paper and sent off to Womach at the Smithsonian, would have to tell his story—helped, of course, by what Don could turn up in his own research about what happened here more than 130 years ago.

Then, on the morning of the fourth day of the dig, Don asked everyone to grab a metal detector and do one final sweep of the ground. It led to a discovery that twenty-two-year-old Janice Page, a graduate student at Maryland, would never forget. Neither would Don.

She waved her metal detector over the empty grave itself, something nobody—including Don—had thought to do once the remains had been removed. Several inches in the ground directly below where the bones and artifacts had been, she followed up on a detector ping. She sifted out a round piece of metal about the size of a quarter. There was engraved writing on both sides, a tiny hole near the edge. A coin? Yes, that must be it. She had found some kind of coin. Or was it something else?

"Doctor Spaniel!" she yelled. "I have something!"

He was there on his knees by her side in a flash. Yes, she had something all right.

At a glance, he knew what she had. It was an ID disk! A Civil War version of the dog tags worn by American service personnel and made most famous during World War Two.

Don Spaniel took that little round object into his right hand as if it were the Hope Diamond.

He had examined many Civil War ID disks. Most were made of lead or, even better, brass so that they would not corrode or otherwise deteriorate.

This one was brass. It had not deteriorated.

The whole team, now absolutely silent, gathered around him and Janice Page.

They watched as he grabbed a tiny hard-bristle brush and slowly, carefully stroked one side of the disk. Then he took a magnifying glass out of his shirt pocket, held the disk under it, and moved them up to within inches of his right eye.

"War of 1861," he read in a loud voice. "United States."

Somebody in the team said, "Oh, boy." He was the only one who spoke. Most were holding their breath.

Don turned the disk over. He repeated with the brush what he had done to the other side. He whisked it clean as if he were performing eye or brain surgery. He again put it under his magnifying glass.

Then he read in a slow voice what was on that side of the disk: "T. L. Flintson. Twenty-third Massachusetts Volunteers. Saint Paul."

A cheer went up from the team.

Don Spaniel stood up.

"We know who he is," he proclaimed to his happy group.

It was a confident announcement but not one that inspired him to shout. The truth was, Don would have preferred much more of a search. This was too simple—too easy.

Henry Milliken, one of the relic hunters who had found the remains, was delighted about the recovery of the ID disk.

"How long does that mean then that it'll be before the artifacts—you know, the pistol and the other stuff we took out of the grave—might be released?"

Don, appalled at the man's self-serving reaction, said he had no idea about when the items would be available. And he suddenly wished he had not followed his impulse to come into this place called Antietam Memories. He wanted to race right back outside to his waiting crew and van and get the hell out of here.

The shop was in the center of Sharpsburg, a one-main-street town of not quite a thousand people and small frame houses that didn't look much different than it had 134 years ago. Don knew from the park-police officers that the store was run by one of the relic hunters who found the remains. *Doesn't he deserve to be told the good news, too, that we have just identified the dead man as T. L. Flintson of the Twenty-third Massachusetts?*

Don had whipped his lime-green Park Service Jeep Cherokee SUV into a parking space in front of the store and jumped out, telling his colleagues that he would be only a minute.

There was a jingle of a bell when Don opened the door and was quickly greeted by Milliken coming from the back of the store. He was dressed in khaki trousers and a gray sweatshirt decorated with crossed Union and Confederate flags—in full color.

After Don resisted the urge to flee, Milliken insisted on showing Don around his establishment. It was a two-story house that the Union army had used to billet wounded soldiers for several weeks after the battle of Antietam.

"We've got a little bit of something for everybody," said Milliken, who spoke with a tight drawl that Don recognized as native western Maryland. Don was no Professor Higgins, but his ear for accent and dialogue was fairly good.

The store's three large downstairs rooms were nothing less than a commercial shrine to the men and battle of Antietam. On the walls were framed oil paintings and prints of young men in blue and gray charging one another, bayoneting one another, shooting one another. Some were on foot, others were on horseback, still others were lying on the ground holding their hands over bleeding stomachs and chests. There were portraits, both photographs and paintings, of Lee, McClellan, Burnside, Stonewall Jackson, A. P. Hill, and lesser combatants. One wall was covered with a variety of unit flags and battle maps, including one three feet by five feet that was a reprint of an official one drawn by the U.S. Army immediately after the battle. There were some thirty to forty authentic muskets and other long rifles displayed neatly in polished-wood racks that were mounted along another wall.

Don peered down into several glass display cases, the kind found in jewelry stores. They were teeming with a mixture of real items from the battlefield as well as replicas. The relics were workable pistols, and also canteens, knives, buckles, and buttons, as well as spent pistol and rifle bullets, insignia and emblems, and remnants of shoes and boots. Don's eyes lingered for more than a few seconds on a half-dozen brass ID disks that had prices on them from five hundred to one thousand dollars each.

The new stuff included toy soldiers made of lead, wood, and plastic, as well as pewter ashtrays of Burnside Bridge, coffee mugs, T-shirts, baseball caps, beach towels, and blankets emblazoned with battle scenes and other Antietam images. Don also browsed several open shelves of Antietam and Civil War books, CDs, videotapes of movies and TV programs, posters, board games, jigsaw puzzles. . . .

Indeed, a little bit of something for everybody.

Don was about to say his good-byes when he spotted a sign over a closed door in the back: THE SUTLERY—FOR REENACTORS.

"Everything in there is one hundred percent authentic," said Henry Milliken, motioning for Don to have a look.

Don knew enough about the reenacting world to know that *authentic* was a serious word. Most reenactors spared no expense or effort in assuring the historic accuracy of their equipment and uniforms. *Sutlery* was the Civil War–era term for stores and wagons where troops could buy food, tobacco, clothes, and other provisions.

Milliken's sutlery was about the size of three walk-in closets. More than a dozen dark blue Union uniform coats and light blue trousers of varying styles hung on a wooden clothes rack against the left wall, a similar selection of Confederate gray coats and butternut pants on the right. Above each on narrow shelves were ten or so uniform hats, emblems, and insignias, plus a combination of kepis and slouch hats, several pairs of long underwear, and an array of canteens, haversacks, and leather belts. Don also recognized small packages of hardtack, the mainstay cracker of Civil War combatants. On the floor beneath the hanging uniforms were leather and canvas boots and shoes. Everything here was serious stuff, carefully made to replicate what the real soldiers in the real Civil War had worn and used.

"There's a woman over at Harpers Ferry who makes our uniforms," said Milliken. "She and her husband, who is a top reenactor, use nothing but the right materials—down to the cloth, thread, stitching, and every other detail."

Impressed, Don shook his head.

"I'll bet you've never had one of these uniforms on, have you?"

Don nodded slightly.

"What are you—about a forty-two long?" said Milliken.

Don nodded again. "Very long, yes."

"Reb or Yank?" asked Milliken.

Don Spaniel had grown up in Virginia, so his first loyalty had been entirely to the Confederate side. But now, without a thought, he said, "Yank." It must have had something to do with T. L. Flintson of the Twenty-third Massachusetts. . . .

Milliken asked, "What about this?" He had grabbed a dark blue wool single-breasted frock coat off the rack. Don recognized the rank-insignia shoulder boards as those of a lieutenant and also saw the price in large black numbers on a white tag: $220.

From behind, as if he were a haberdasher, Milliken fitted Don's long arms into the Union lieutenant's coat and then adjusted the shoulders. Through his shirt, Don felt the comfort of a black polished-cotton lining. The eight gold buttons were heavy—authentic. He buttoned four of them down his front. The sleeves were slightly too short, but other than that it was a pretty good fit.

Milliken grabbed a Union officer's kepi, a cap patterned after those of the French military that became standard headgear for both sides in the Civil War. It was a small, round, billed cap that sloped forward from a rear peak.

Don took the kepi and walked to a full-length mirror against the far wall. He put the kepi on his head. The gold braided quatrefoil for a first lieutenant on top of the round hat was most impressive.

"All you need is a mustache and you could lead a charge down a hill," said Milliken.

That remark made Don uncomfortable. He felt some warmth in his face as he looked at himself. In all of his now more than ten years dealing with the archeology and the residue of the Civil War, this was the first time he had actually done anything like this. Never before had he imagined himself in a blue or gray uniform, leading a charge down anything. *Here I am, all dressed up like a Union soldier. And I don't look too bad. The man's right.*

"Let me show you something else," Milliken said, pointing to a small, gray metal door behind the Union uniform rack. "That's my little armory. A lieutenant's got to have the right kind of weapon."

Using a large key on a key ring, he unlocked the door, reached inside, and pulled out a handgun. Don recognized it immediately as an 1860 army .44-caliber revolver. He had seen these newly made firearms before at Civil War trade shows and in the hands of reenactors. They were truly exact working replicas of the ones used by both Union and Confederate officers—lieutenants such as the man on the hillside they now knew to be T. L. Flintson of the Twenty-third Massachusetts. The price tag on the gun was $174.

"A thing of beauty is what it is, isn't it?" Milliken asked.

Don Spaniel took the revolver in his two hands, held it for a count of five, and returned it to Milliken. "Yes, sir."

"Here's some hardtack—on me," said Milliken, handing Don a white cardboard package of what appeared to contain about ten of the thick three-inch-square crackers made of unleavened wheat flour and water. A tiny sticker put the price for the pack at eight dollars.

Don considered whether it would be a violation of some government code of ethics to accept a gift worth eight dollars from Henry Milliken. He concluded it might be but decided it would be professionally worthy—and fun—to sample the taste of hardtack anyhow.

He removed the kepi from his head and began to take off the dark blue coat.

"We sell and sometimes rent all of this stuff," said Henry Milliken, helping Don with the coat. "But anytime, for any reason you'd like to borrow anything here, all you have to do is ask."

The offer seemed strange, inappropriate to Don. He couldn't imagine a situation ever arising in which he would want to dress up as a Civil War soldier.

The next evening, just as everyone was leaving for the day, the research assistant assigned to tracking Flintson came to Don's office with an announcement.

"We have a problem," said Marjorie Reston. "The Twenty-third Massachusetts was not at Burnside Bridge—not even at Antietam, not even in another part of the battle, not at Bloody Lane, not in the West Woods beyond the Dunker Church, not in the East Woods—"

"Where were they?"

"They were in North Carolina on September 17, 1862."

"The guy might have been on headquarters assignment and was sent to deliver a message or an order to somebody. Maybe he was a replacement," Don said. "Keep checking; you'll find out what he was doing there."

Marjorie Reston shook her head. Her bright blond hair didn't move because there wasn't much of it. She wore it closely cropped, shorter than many men—such as Reg Womach, for example. She was a large woman of thirty-five who, unlike most of Don's other staff members, wore the dark green uniform of the National Park Service to work every day. That meant Spaniel had never seen her in anything but trousers and, frankly, never wanted or expected otherwise. Faye Lee Sutton, the Interior Department attorney, wasn't the only in-house or work-related woman he had allowed his wandering eye to linger upon, and he had even had low-octane dates with a couple of his coworkers in the past. But the wandering had led only to a quick glance when it came to Marjorie. What he wanted from her, and always received, was the quickest and most thorough research possible.

"Come on, there could be all kinds of explanations," he said in response to her head shake. "Not everything about the Army of the Potomac was perfectly orderly or well organized."

"There's another thing that's even more . . . well, more of a problem, Doctor Spaniel," she said. "T. L. Flintson of the Twenty-third Massachusetts is buried in a cemetery alongside his mother and father in Saint Paul, Massachusetts."

"Now *that* is what I call a problem," said Don. "But can we be certain he is really buried there?"

"Yes, I think we can. For one thing, U.S. military records at the National Archives show that he was reported wounded on March 14, 1862, in the battle of Newberne and died seventeen days later in a hospital in Newberne—now New Berne—North Carolina. His date of death was March 31, 1862, more than five months before the battle of Antietam."

She removed a piece of paper from a folder and handed it to Don. "Here is the real proof. I just got this from the Library of Congress."

It was a photocopy of a story about the funeral of T. L. Flintson from the April 4, 1862, edition of the Saint Paul *Pantagraph*.

Don, in his puzzled excitement, read the last two paragraphs out loud. " 'His grieving mother, father, and two sisters were at his bedside at the hospital in Newberne when he died. They traveled by boat with their fallen loved one's remains on the long journey home to the Massachusetts soil from which he had sprung and to which he would now return.

" 'The young hero was laid to rest in his full uniform with sword. All citizens of Saint Paul viewed him in his finery before he was placed to his final rest.' "

They saw him! T. L. Flintson's remains are in Massachusetts, not in Reg Womach's lab at the Smithsonian!

But how did his ID disk end up in the grave of another man who died somewhere else five months later?

Don Spaniel was thinking—and smiling. Suddenly, he and his team and their world of archeological/anthropological mystery were back in business.

"We still don't know who he is!" he shouted at Marjorie Reston and everyone else in the office.

And he picked up the phone and shouted it again to his friend Reg Womach at the Smithsonian Institution.

"So it's back to work on the bones," said Reg. "I had already done some preliminary stuff before that disk showed up. . . ."

"It's full speed ahead now," Don said.

"Got it. How about meeting me for a drink? We can go down the street from here to the bar at the Willard."

"I've got work to do, and so do you, for God's sake," Don said, hanging up the phone. How could Reg even consider something like that at a time like this?

Don left the office at the same time as Marjorie Reston and his other colleagues, but even as he was driving his car across the Fourteenth Street Bridge, his mind continued to race elsewhere.

If you're not T. L. Flintson of the Twenty-third Massachusetts, then who in the hell are you, sir?

Colonel Doleman had said the first evidence pointed toward one of the Connecticut regiments. Most likely the Eleventh. Most probably not the tragic Sixteenth, the one shot to pieces in the cornfield. That happened on the other side of the Antietam. The Eleventh was right there. But so were Pennsylvania and New York units. *The Eleventh. Yes, I will begin with the Eleventh. I have to start somewhere. . . .*

He had a modest personal collection of Civil War books at his apartment. They included the basics—Catton, Foote, McPherson, Furgurson—plus several biographies and diaries of the best-known generals, atlases, and battle maps, as well as specialty almanacs on both sides' military chains of command, uniforms, firearms, and other equipment.

His apartment was on the second floor of a three-story condo just past the Pentagon in Shirlington, part of the close-in Virginia suburb of Arlington. He had lived there almost five years, but he barely paid any attention to it. There were two bedrooms, but only one of them had a bed. He used the other as a store-room and as a place for his once-a-week cleaning woman to do some ironing. There was also a living room, a bathroom, and a kitchen. The refrigerator and the bread box, where he kept some food and drink necessities, were the principal tools of his home life. The furniture, all bought at the same store in about thirty minutes, was cheap, pine, and virtually invisible. The walls were bare except for a large print of some wild horses in the ocean surf of the Maryland coast that his visiting mother, appalled at the sparseness, had bought at a nearby frame and art shop. This place—and you, son—need a woman's touch, she said repeatedly. And he repeatedly responded, Someday, yes.

He went right to the books on the shelf in the living room, pulled down the "Fort Sumter to Perryville" volume of Shelby Foote's narrative of the Civil War, and turned to his account of the battle of Antietam. It was the one Colonel Doleman had quoted the other day.

There was no mention of the Eleventh Connecticut. But Foote wrote that General Burnside was so fascinated with the bridge that he didn't test the water's depth. "If he had, he would have discovered that the copper-covered stream, less than fifty feet in width, could have been waded at almost any point without wetting the armpits of the shortest man in his corps."

In a fast search through indexes and tables of contents in any McPherson or Furgurson, he could find nothing specific about the Eleventh. He had a book that showed colored pictures of Union officers' uniforms, but it was vague about what styles were worn by the Connecticut regiments.

Clearly, this was going to require a serious research mission to Carlisle, to the U.S. Army Military History Institute. He would set it up tomorrow.

Then, in a book on Civil War arms, he found confirmation of something he already knew about the .44 Army Colt's being used by many Union officers. The photograph of one actually carried by such an officer in the battle of Gettysburg looked exactly like the one Don had held in his hands in Milliken's sutlery. But, as he stared at the half-page photo more intently, he began to question whether it was the same model as the rusted one found in the hillside grave.

Wait a minute.

On the next page was a photo of a similar revolver identified as a .44 *Police* Colt model. "This firearm was never officially issued to officers but was a common gift to them by members of their families and friends as they went off to war," said the caption underneath. "It was slightly lighter and smaller than the more commonly used .44 Army Colt."

Could *that* be what the hillside man's revolver was? Most probably, yes.

The thought brought a wave of well-being through him. Realizations such as this, no matter how small, were what made Don Spaniel a happy man. It may not matter to anybody else—or ultimately even be helpful in his search for the identity of the man on the Antietam hillside—but knowing it was a *Police* Colt rather than an *Army* Colt brought him exquisite pleasure.

Later, as he closed his eyes to go to sleep, his last thoughts were about how grateful he was to have found archeology as a way to make a living—and to live a life that was full of such extraordinary pleasures.

And he also hoped to hell Reg Womach had gone right back to work on those bones.

In December we were transported by train to New York City, where the Eleventh Connecticut was presented its official colors: a blue flag with accents of gold, purple, and white. An army general made the presentation in a brief formation ceremony that, to my unfulfilled expectations, was without the song, color, or majesty that I believed the occasion demanded. But, as Joseph Campbell, one of the seven other good men of East Preston in our company, said to my complaint: "Making you sergeant, Albert, did not make you in charge of the whole Union army." I replied: "They could have done worse." It was a statement that lay bare a youth's high level of esteem and admiration, at which I held myself at that moment.

Only a few days later, we were dispatched on a steamer to Annapolis, Maryland, on the Chesapeake Bay and from there on toward another place I knew only by name, the State of North Carolina. We were finally going south to meet the enemy.

Most of the events during those first weeks and months of 1862 are irrelevant to my present accounting, and a few, if recounted here, would do no good to the historical reputation of those people, mostly U.S. military officers of considerable rank, who were involved. The worst happening, which I truly will not detail, was the embarrassment of our steamer running aground far off the coast of North Carolina, a development that left us adrift and unable to disembark or be useful as a military unit for more than thirty days!

It was not until March of 1862 that we had our first encounter with Rebel forces in what was later to be called the battle of Newberne in North Carolina. Even then, most of us in the Eleventh Connecticut saw no Rebel soldiers nor fired a shot in anything resembling anger. Joseph Campbell was the only one of us from East Preston to become a casualty from the action. He was hit hard in his right hip by a piece of cast iron that apparently came from one of the canisters the Rebs were stuffing with any and all pieces of scrap metal and then firing out of their cannons to rain down on us.

Campbell returned from several days at a field hospital in the town of Newberne with an account of his experience there that was so horrendously nightmarish that I prayed to my God from that nightfall on that if I be felled by a Reb ball or shot, please, my Father in Heaven, take me quickly and thus spare me the agony of a suffering death such as Campbell witnessed. He spoke of screams from the wounded and dying that resembled the cries of wild animals. He said it was those sounds that gave him the strength and will to leave that awful place and to return here to our unit, to his comrades. He vowed that he would not spend his last days screaming as an animal to a god who clearly was not listening anyhow. He said he meant no offense to me, Albert Randolph, and to others who hold that God is always listening and is good and only good.

"Good is a word that comes from the word god, Joseph," I replied with calmness and sureness. "They are one in the same." I said no more because I did not feel that the time was opportune for a lengthy discourse on a Listening God. It was just as well be-

cause the experience of Antietam was to bring me thoughts about the goodness of God that I still carry with me.

Campbell's wound healed, and he went north with us to the banks of the Antietam, where the fact of his being in the New-berne field hospital became an important aspect of the story I have drawn my pen to tell.

Reg Womach had gone right to work. He summoned Don to his lab the very next morning, saying, "OK, you bastard, I stayed up half the night with your man's bones. Come and get it."

Don loved coming to this place on the fourth floor of the Smithsonian's National Museum of Natural History. It was as awesome to him as the U.S. Capitol and the Lincoln Memorial at opposite ends of the National Mall. Here Reg Womach, a short, squat forensic anthropologist in blue jeans and with a ponytail, was the majestic one—the king. Here were the master records and skeletons of thirty-four thousand persons who had died in the late nineteenth and early twentieth century. They were the famous Terry Collection, which had come to the Smithsonian on permanent loan from the state of Missouri many years ago. Most of the skeletons, used now for comparison and research purposes, were from archeological sites, but others were there through predeath donation—a kind of forerunner to present-day organ-donation programs. They were kept in metal kitchenlike drawers that were stacked more than ten high in row after row, up near the cluttered offices and labs of Womach and his colleagues.

"I've got some news that will knock your socks off," Reg said upon Don's arrival.

"I'm ready—hit me."

Reg had arranged the bones on a long table in the manner of a skeleton lying facedown—the way they had been found in the dirt at Thaddeus Farm.

"All in good time, doctor. We must go through it all in an orderly manner. These bones ain't going anywhere."

As with the colonel, Don was impatient, but he knew Reg was the best there was at what he did because he was careful and precise as well as absolutely averse to making assumptions. Reg was haunted—and guided—by the well-known single worst assumption story of modern forensic anthropology.

A most prominent man in the field had examined the remains of a perfectly preserved body of an adult male found on top of an opened lead coffin in the vandalized grave of a long-dead Confederate colonel. The full-muscled body was dressed up in a perfectly preserved uniform, with polished boots, a sword, and other paraphernalia of a Confederate colonel. The famous forensic anthropologist immediately declared the man to have been dead for less than eight hours, opining that the deceased was most likely the victim of a most clever murder by somebody with access to a full array of Confederate artifacts. As the police raced off in search of a murderer, the expert went on to take a closer and more complete examination of the body. Whoops, he declared in a few days. The remains really are those of the Confederate colonel. He was so well preserved because of the special nature of the lead coffin in which he had been buried. Authorities speculated afterward that the grave had been opened by some real grave robbers in search of some choice Confederate war relics. They had expected to find skeletal remains and maybe a few buttons, a sword, and possibly a rusted pistol. Instead, there lay a body of somebody who looked like he had just been put there. They had panicked and run. Thus was born the BORC rule of life in the small world of forensic anthropology: Beware Of (W)Rong Colonel.

Reg asked Don to stand on one side of the table while he remained on the other. Thus, they took on the appearance of two poorly dressed doctors on hospital rounds.

"Please observe," Reg began, "that almost all of the normal human body's two hundred and six name-bearing bones are present and accounted for."

"So observed," Don said, obviously without actually counting any of them.

"They are of a male, so proved by features of the cranium— prominent supramastoid crest and external occipital protuberance and the size and shape of the chin, or mandible—and the overall size of the rest of the skeleton. The length of the clavicles, size of the femoral heads, and size and shape of the pelvis are typically male."

This really is going to take a while, thought Don. *But as with Colonel Doleman, so be it.*

"Age, twenty-one to thirty years. So determined by a lot of things such as good bone joints—joint surfaces generally free of osteoarthritis. Healthy arm and leg bones—complete closure of long-bone epiphyses—and a solid cranium and teeth that show the kind of wear consistent with somebody that age.

"Height, five feet eleven inches; weight, one hundred seventy pounds. The height was determined by measuring the femurs. The weight was calculated by a rough formula based on the size of and wear and tear on the bones.

"Lifestyle. Condition of teeth indicate someone who cared about neatness and orderliness. The teeth plus health of bones generally point toward no deprivation, no poverty. The man most likely ate and otherwise lived well and had done so his entire life. The bones showed signs of his being involved in vigorous physical pursuits such as athletic games."

Don's socks remained very much in place. *Onward, please, Reg!*

"Special characteristics that could be used for positive ID? Indications of mild back problems—there are unusually shaped anterior borders of some of the thoracic vertebrae. And the fact that our man here suffered a broken left arm when he was twelve to fourteen years old."

"How in the hell do you know that, Reg?"

"The left humerus has a healed break in it, that is how I know. It was a thin one, and it had healed so completely I almost missed it. But under the magnifying glass it's obvious."

He reached down, picked up the left humerus bone, handed it and a large magnifying glass toward Don. "Want to see for yourself?"

Don declined with a hand gesture and said, "So he clearly wasn't hampered by it in any way. Otherwise, he couldn't have been in the army."

"He was fine. It broke, and it healed back quite normally. I would be surprised if at the time of his death he had anything but full use of his left arm."

Don was delighted to know anything new about their man. But then, on second thought, he couldn't immediately put it into a helpful category. "I don't know how that helps us, Reg, to be completely honest about it. I hope this wasn't your big news."

"Find the name of somebody who died at Burnside Bridge who was a boxer, a horseman, or a wrestler, or fell out of a tree when he was a kid and you've got your man."

"Great, Reg. Thanks a lot."

Reg smiled. "Let's go on to the wrists."

The wrists?

"A combination of rust stains and residue and a slight indentation in the carpal bones of both wrists gives strong indication that the wrists had been tied together by something metallic, possibly steel wire, either at or just before death and burial."

Bull's-eye. "Hey, Reg!"

"Hey, yes, Don! Most probably tied behind his back!"

Don suddenly remembered something that had been found with the remains. A small metal buckle, less than an inch square. There was the slight trace of leather around one of the edges. It was too small for a belt buckle. He had assumed—but had yet to confirm—that it was a buckle from a knapsack strap. He knew it to be a common style worn by soldiers on both sides. He had wondered at the time about the rest of the knapsack. Why would there be only a lone strap buried with that man at Burnside?

He now said to Womach, "Are those metallic marks consistent with a metal buckle on a strap of some kind?"

"Could be, you bet. A small buckle. Nothing huge."

"You're a genius, Doctor Womach," said Doctor Spaniel.

"I know," said Reg.

Don really did think Reginald Lucas Womach was a genius. At the age of forty-two, Reg was the forensic anthropologist to which law-enforcement officers and others brought their most difficult identification mysteries. He had done work on the long-buried bones of people who had been mutilated by crazed killers and of former presidents and other celebrities—movie stars, bank robbers, billionaire bankers—whose cause of death had suddenly become of new interest.

Don loved Reg's tale of how he got interested in the bones business. There was a most unusual graveyard in Medora, a tiny Old

West town fifty miles west of Dickinson, North Dakota, his hometown. A few of the tombstones had no names, only descriptions. One said: "Baby From Hotel." Another: "U.S. Army Soldier From Cantonment, Fell From R.R. Bridge." Reg, taken there many times by relatives and on school history trips, had a favorite: "Man The Bank Fell On."

"Now for the real socks information," Reg said to Don, reaching for the skull. "Cause of death: a bullet shot through the skull from back to front. The shot entered below the lateral/medial pterygoid plates and exited through the frontal glabella three millimeters above the nasal cavity."

Reg held the skull up between him and Don.

"This is an exit wound," he said, pointing to the one in the front.

He turned the skull around. "This is an entrance wound back here."

"You're sure about this?"

"No question about it. There was even a small piece of the bullet stuck there in the front hole."

Reg set the skull back down and motioned for Spaniel to join him at a nearby table and look into a microscope. There was a slide in the aperture and several others stacked beside it.

"That's a blowup of the entrance hole, and it's clean as a whistle," Reg said.

Don looked and agreed. There was nothing there but the hole.

Reg changed the slide. "Now, this one."

Don saw through the microscope a similar hole but with a piece of something on one edge. "What does it all really say, Reg?" he asked, although he was pretty sure where all of this was headed.

Reg said: "This man was shot from behind, the bullet following an upward angle."

"Meaning he was lying facedown, the way he was found in that grave?"

"Possibly—yes."

"With his hands tied behind him!"

"Could be. Execution style. If so, the question for you, my friend, is: Why would somebody—presumably the Confederates—have executed this man right there on the battlefield?"

"I've never heard of anything like that. There were some bloody massacres, but nothing quite like this." Then after a few beats of silence, he added in an angry whisper, "My God, Reg."

And he slammed a ballpoint pen down hard on the table.

"Hey, hey, Don," said Reg. "Get a grip—whatever anybody did to this guy, it was done in 1862. OK?"

Don let it pass. But Reg knew damn well that Don's archeological emotions were never tempered by how long ago something had happened. In fact, the more ancient, the stronger he felt!

Reg said, "Remember that we've a part of a bullet to work with. It could help identify the type of weapon used."

"What kind of bullet was it?" Don barked.

"Calm down, will you? There's not enough there for me to tell. Only a real ballistics man—one of the FBI lab types—could tell you that, and even he might not be able to. Were any traces of bullets found on your dig around the remains?"

"No. Will you find the right FBI type?"

Reg said sure and suggested they go over to one of the restaurants at the National Gallery for an early lunch.

"No way," said Don. "There's work to do. *Both* of us have work to do. Call the FBI—"

"I'll call them, but I might not go over there—for obvious reasons."

Don just nodded. He knew Reg did not want to take a chance of running into his former wife, Susan, an FBI forensic specialist on human hair who was now married to an FBI chemist. They had worked closely on the famous Ralph Joe Hopkins serial-murder case in Mississippi, and when Susan returned from several hard days and nights examining the body parts of the eight dismembered teenage girls, she had announced her love for her FBI colleague and asked Reg for a divorce.

"Hey, Don. I did my BORC testing, I know this guy's already been dead for more than one hundred and thirty years. What's the hurry?"

Don rushed out the door without answering.

And very shortly afterward, back at his own office, he ran into another kind of door.

"Denied—not urgent, for God's sake" was written across the top of his memo to the regional administrator. Don had requested permission to miss the monthly staff planning meeting on Friday to do some *urgent* research on the "Burnside remains matter" at Carlisle.

Don, in a fury, barged into the administrator's outer office and announced at the top of his lungs to a startled secretary: "I will be sick with a heart attack Friday! Sick leave! Count it as sick leave!"

The other important Antietam relevancies of those early days in 1862 were the coming to us of General Ambrose Burnside and Colonel Henry Kingsbury. Burnside, for whom our fateful bridge across the Antietam would later be named, was commander of the Ninth Corps, of which our Eleventh Connecticut Volunteers was made a part. He carried a reputation for pomposity and incompetence that would be improper to pass on in detail even now. His actions at Antietam are those that matter to this chronicle, so his reputation prior to that serves only to confirm many an early forecast that the Ninth Corps was to be poorly led by this man from Indiana who wore his chin whiskers in a peculiar flourish from his head hair down the sides of both cheeks. Some were heard to remark that his facial hair, later to be mimicked and nicknamed "sideburns," was his sole positive contribution to the American way of life. I have no reason to challenge such an assertion.

Our beloved Colonel Kingsbury, on the other hand, was everything General Burnside was not, or vice versa. He came to us that summer as commanding officer of the Eleventh, having once already declined to command our regiment. As a West Point graduate and professional soldier, he had hoped for the command of a regular army unit rather than one of volunteers. But when implored a second time to command our Eleventh, his loyalty to his home state of Connecticut rose up and overcame his own personal wishes. As a native son of our own soil, having been born and brought to manhood in the Connecticut village of Lyme, he could not resist the clear and urgent need we had for his strong and firm and devoted leadership. By the time he came to us in July of 1862, we were at Newport News, Virginia, and a part of the Army of the Potomac preparing for the major Union push northward into Maryland in pursuit of General Lee and his Army of Northern Virginia.

Colonel Kingsbury was twenty-five years old, but even to my eighteen-year-old eyes and mind he was a man of substance and maturity. His hair, his mustache were blond and graceful; his eyes were blue, welcoming. His face and body, his demeanor, his bearing transmitted physical and mental strength.

To say that we needed him is to say something so obvious as to be on a par with exclaiming about the connection between rain and a puddle in a muddy roadway. I will spare the details, but I must declare that we were not well led nor trained before. The junior officers, including a Captain John Griswold, also of Lyme, as well as our own Lieutenant Allbritten, did what they could to push their respective boulders of responsibility up various hills, but the higher-ranking officers did not.

Colonel Kingsbury immediately began putting our entire regiment into military order. It was truly remarkable how soon he turned us into a unit of great efficiency, inspiring us with a confidence in his leadership that was little short of devotion. He visited the tents in the night to see that the men were properly cared for, and he gave instruction for the preparation of the food, ordering solid breakfasts and light suppers and instructing the cook in the use of rice and ordering him to prepare tenderloin steaks, which were reserved for the officers, for the men because he demanded that his men must be fed as well as his officers.

I was the personal subject of an anecdote that made the rounds. Colonel Kingsbury inspected me very minutely one afternoon and, despite my having accoutred myself with much care, he detected one tarnished button on my cap. "The splendidness of your uniform and presence is highlighted even more by the unshined button, sergeant," he said. "It was wise of you to create such a contrast for me to notice and thus place me in a position to praise your total appearance, which I hereby do." The words of a great and compassionate man!

Colonel Henry Kingsbury made himself a hero and the idol of

his men. Where he would lead, we were ready to follow. Brave, generous, and affectionate, yet calm, cautious, and self-contained, enjoying the fullest confidence of his superiors as well as the devotion of his men, he combined talents that seemed peculiarly to fit him for high military command.

We began the march north with a buoyant belief in ourselves as individual soldiers and as a regiment that ignited our spirits and lightened our steps.

5

For Don Spaniel, being at Carlisle, Pennsylvania, among the books and papers and artifacts of the Army War College's Military History Institute was in a league with his childhood fantasy of spending all day at the Ritz movie theater in Harrisonburg—with an unlimited supply of chocolate-chip ice cream and hot buttered popcorn.

He didn't think much about what he would have done with his life if he had not found archeology, but the only other lines of work that even crossed his mind were those of a high school history teacher or a research professor of some kind. Reg Womach had also told Don more than once that he would have made a good homicide detective. Whatever, reading books and marveling at finding out something new had been parts of what he was since the day he became the first in his fourth-grade class to figure out—from a book found hidden in the back of his parents' library—how males and females went about the business of making babies.

Don had called ahead to arrange for material on the Eleventh Connecticut, as well as the Twenty-third Massachusetts and related Antietam-Burnside matters, to be ready for him. He arrived shortly after ten o'clock in the morning to a most joyful sight on a huge library table in a second-floor room of the institute's old stone building.

There was an array of pamphlets and books, opened or marked with Post-its at relevant sections or chapters. There were letters and diaries—some original, some copies—that had been written by Antietam participants and observers. There were maps, newspaper and magazine articles, photographs, line drawings. . . .

It was a feast of information, waiting for Don to dive in.

He had come with a plan, an approach. He would first try to get an overview understanding of the Eleventh. Colonel Doleman had provided the spirit and the soul of what those young men of the Eleventh had done and what others had done *to* them on September 17, 1862. But he needed much more.

He started grabbing things off the table. He glanced through the carefully marked parts of a huge book on the Connecticut regiments. It was over eight hundred pages, a rah-rah chronicle written in 1868, soon after the war. Then he read some of the pertinent sections in the five-hundred-page *Connecticut for the Union: The Role of the State in the Civil War,* written by historian John Niven and published by Yale University Press in 1965. Next, John Schildt's more modest ninety-four-page book, *Connecticut at Antietam,* which came out in 1988.

Don's brain quickly got crammed, and his hand got cramped from note taking.

But now he knew that the Eleventh's first action was in North Carolina in the spring of 1862. They went on to an encampment on the Trent River and finally to Fredericksburg, Virginia, where they were made a part of the Army of the Potomac. Lincoln had given McClellan command of that army in August 1861 and now ordered him to pursue Lee and his Army of Northern Virginia into Maryland. The Eleventh was in the advance line on the heels of the Rebels through Frederick, Maryland, and then through Fox's Gap, where the Battle of South Mountain was fought. The Confederates fled South Mountain to take up positions along the west bank of the Antietam, a few miles away.

He read from a diary and then a couple of letters. The men and boys of the Eleventh Connecticut clearly had no inkling of the awfulness that lay ahead. Don was touched by the calmness in the account of a young corporal who wrote to his mother the night before South Mountain. He talked about the fragrance of campfires and roasting corn and the sounds of laughing and singing and "watching one of our officers demonstrate the art of personal combat" because he was "skilled in throwing men about, even those who outweigh him by many pounds."

Don continued to skip around, going back to the chronology in a pamphlet published by the U.S. Army twenty years after the war.

After Antietam, the Eleventh went on to participate in eight more battles, all in Virginia, before being part of the triumphant Union march into Richmond in April 1865. The regiment was ordered back to Hartford in November and formally mustered out on December 21, four years and two months after its creation.

"No regiment in the service endured with a more heroic valor the hardships of a four years' war than did the ever glorious old Eleventh," was how an entry on the Eleventh ended in one publication. It was a souvenir bulletin called "The Old Battle Flags" that was put out in 1879 to mark the moving of the Connecticut regiments' battle flags from the State Arsenal to the new state capitol building in Hartford.

From a history of the Eleventh written by a Lieutenant Colonel Charles Warren, Don read:

It has been 33 years since the Connecticut troops faced the Confederates on the hills at Sharpsburg. There have been more spectacular performances in history but no men under similar conditions ever displayed more sublime courage. They fought for neither conquest, glory nor the immediate protection of the fields upon which they had been reared. Sustained only by their ideal of eternal justice, faraway from their native hearthstones, they submerged the individual in zeal for the nation.

Yes, sir! Don felt warmth—and a strange sense of pride in the men of the Eleventh.

He jumped to the reading of a soldier's dispatch in the September 24, 1862, Hartford *Weekly Post* that engaged in some Reb bashing and wishful thinking: "Bah. Is there any honor in beating insanity? Perhaps not. But there is glory in muzzling madness, which I think McClellan intends to do with the two to three thousand muzzles he has in hand."

Don came close to yelling out: "Sorry, soldier! Not this time. McClellan did nothing with those muzzles!"

His attention danced on to a page toward the end of that eight-hundred-page book he had perused earlier. It was a tally sheet summarizing the Eleventh's total casualties. The regiment had had a tragic and bloody war. Eighty-eight—including the twenty-nine at Burnside Bridge—were killed outright in combat. Another fifty-three died later from wounds, fifty-four died in Confederate prisons, and 109 others died of disease. The number of wounded who survived was 319.

But of particular interest was the last item. "Unaccounted for at muster-out: 30." Thirty young men of Connecticut who went away with the Eleventh Regiment were unaccounted for when it was all over.

Could one of them be the man in the grave on that high ground above Burnside Bridge?

Don made a note to see if the National Archives had a list of those thirty unaccounted-fors.

Back to some letters. There were several from George Lewis Bronson, a hospital steward in the Eleventh Connecticut. Covering four years of his war experience, they were written to his wife back in Berlin, Connecticut, in a meticulous handwriting that was as steady and straight as the stories it told.

There was even one dated September 17, 1862. He wrote—all of his letters started "Dear Wife"—that his regiment had been ordered to take the bridge and hold it so that the division could pass over.

And he said: "I do not know the name of the creek, but I have named it the creek of death. Such slaughter I hope never to witness again. The fight was very severe."

Four days later, on the twenty-first, he wrote a longer letter describing what had happened.

The loss of the Eleventh is dreadful. . . .

I followed in the rear of the regiment until it reached the fatal bridge that crosses the creek. This bridge is composed of three stone arches, and the stream is about the size of that one just west of Berlin. The enemy's sharpshooters commenced the action, being posted in trees and under cover of a wall on the high ground on the other side of the creek. . . .

The action soon became general all along the lines. Language would fail me to describe the scene. . . .

I can assure you the way the bullets whistled around is better imagined than described. The shells also bursting over our heads and on the ground around us . . .

I took off my coat to dress wounds and met with a great loss.

Some villain rifled my pockets and took several packages of medicine, my fine-tooth comb and what I valued most, my needle book containing the little lock of hair you put in.

Don read George Lewis Bronson's Antietam descriptions several times and then asked an archivist for photocopies.

And he went on to a 183-page report of an Army War College "study project" entitled, "Battlefield Terrain Study: Burnside's Attack Against the Confederate Right at Antietam." The author was a War College student at the time—May 1985—named Lieutenant Colonel John D. Fuller.

Don assumed that by now he already knew most of what must be in the document, but he couldn't help himself. He had to read it, experience it—one more time.

The whole story was there, told through postbattle reports of the generals and other officers and enlisted men on both sides. The most cogent words of summary from the Union perspective were these of Jacob Cox, one of Burnside's generals:

It was now about one o'clock, and nearly three hours had been spent in a bitter and bloody contest across the narrow stream. The successive efforts to carry the bridge had been as closely following each other as possible. Each had been a fierce combat, in which the men with wonderful courage had not easily accepted defeat, and even, when not able to cross the bridge, had made use of the walls at the end, the fences, and every tree and stone as cover, as they strove to reach with their fire their well-protected and nearly concealed opponents. The lulls in the fighting had been short, and only to prepare new efforts. The severity of the work was attested by our losses, which, before the crossing was won, exceeded five hundred men, and included some of our best officers, such as Colonel Kingsbury of the Eleventh Connecticut.

Colonel Henry Walter Kingsbury of Lyme, Connecticut. Don stopped reading and went through a box of photos on the table. There he was. It was a full-length standing portrait of Kingsbury that was taken after his graduation from West Point. Colonel Doleman had said Kingsbury was a man with blue eyes and a mustache. The photo, of course, was black and white, so the eye color was impossible to discern. But there was that mustache, heavy and brushed. Milliken had been right about a mustache being a statement of command, bearing. Don saw in the photo an uncommon look of physical and mental strength. It helped Don understand why the men of the Eleventh followed him down that hillside into the face of Confederate shells and shot.

Don jerked back to the War College student's report. He read one long sentence from the battle report of General Toombs, the Confederate commander: "At between 9 and 10 o'clock the enemy made his first attempt to carry the bridge by a rapid assault, and was repulsed with great slaughter, and at irregular intervals, up to about 1 o'clock, made four other attempts of some kind, all of which were gallantly met and repulsed."

Don picked up a picture book. *Antietam: A Photographic Legacy of America's Bloodiest Day,* which was published in 1978. The author, William Frassanito, had assembled some of the ninety-five photographs taken immediately after the battle by two former associates of the famous Mathew Brady.

Then he set the book back down and read through an article about the photos in the magazine *Civilization.* The pictures had been put on exhibition in Mathew Brady's second-floor gallery at Tenth and Broadway in New York City in October 1862. Wrote a reporter in *The New York Times,* "Crowds of people are constantly going up the stairs. Follow them and you find them bending over photographic views of that fearful battle-field, taken immediately after the action. There is a terrible fascination about it that draws one near these pictures and makes them loath to leave them."

The visitors brought magnifying glasses to look even closer at what the *Civilization* writer, Michael Kernan, described as "pictures of anonymous young men, grimy and bloated in death, on rows of post-card-sized album cards in glass display cases."

Don, without thinking about it, immediately borrowed a magnifying glass from one of the institute archivist-historians. He placed it over those clear black-and-white photos of dead young men, some lain out in imprecise rows, others lying on top of one another, apparently where they fell. Some of the bodies had already begun to swell. Several had arms extended upward by rigor mortis.

Don saw sweat and dirt on foreheads, fear and peace in eyes. He saw pockets that had been turned wrong-side out by a looting soldier. He saw bullet holes in stomachs, sides, and heads, shirts, pants, and jackets.

He saw mouths frozen wide open.

Those photos stirred the people in New York in October 1862 as they stirred a thirty-seven-year-old archeologist at a library table 134 years later.

Don imagined sweat on his own forehead and dirt on his cheeks; he felt pain from a hole in his chest, from the bloating of his own stomach. That smell of death Colonel Doleman had provoked on the battlefield the other day came pouring up now from the pages of the Frassanito book as if, following the practice of perfumed fashion magazines, someone had sprayed odors of blood and urine and gunpowder and filth onto the pages.

He opened his mouth and held it open for a few seconds,

closed his eyes, took several deep breaths, and waited for the awfulness to pass. It may have been as many as two minutes before he could continue.

When he finally turned the page, there before him was a photograph taken from the vantage point of the Eleventh. The place where he and the colonel had walked. Yes, that was it! The caption under it read: "Burnside Bridge, view looking westward across the ground over which Union forces charged, Gardner, stereo #600, September 21, 1862." Gardner was Alexander Gardner, the photographer who had worked for Mathew Brady.

In the text, Frassanito noted that it showed the scene "as it appeared to the members of the Eleventh Connecticut as they dashed frantically toward the creek amid a hail of enemy rifle fire issuing from the wooded heights beyond."

Don put his magnifying glass over every piece of that photograph. He kept it there so long that he began, as he had with Colonel Doleman, to see those kids from the Eleventh Connecticut dashing across that open field. Don was there again.

But soon he was back looking at the huge 1868 book, *The Military and Civil History of Connecticut During the War of 1861–65,* by W. A. Croffut and John M. Morris. He zipped to a version of how Captain Griswold of the Eleventh, the man who had jumped into the creek, actually died, an account that sounded more fable than fact.

It was written by a surgeon named Meyer who said he and four privates waded across the Antietam and retrieved Griswold's bleeding body from the bank.

The surgeon wrote:

We took him into a low shed near the bank, and laid him on the straw. The gallant fellow, sensitive as a Roman to the exhibition of pain, like a Roman had covered his face. When I removed the handkerchief, he was ashy pale, so much had he suffered.

"Doctor," he said, "pardon the trouble I give you, but I am mortally wounded, I believe."

I examined. The bullet had passed through the body in the region of the stomach. "You are, captain," I replied.

"Then let me die quickly, and without pain, if you can," he rejoined. "I am perfectly happy, doctor. This is the death I have always wished to die. Not even the pains of this body can make me unhappy. But oh!"—

Here another spasm of suffering came on. I gave him some morphine. He felt easier. Seeing through the door of the shed the blue water flash in the sunshine, he repeated the first lines of one of those gems of Horace we had so often admired:

> "O Tons Bandusiae, splendidor vitro,
> Dulci digno mero, non sine floribus."

Captain Griswold, according to the doctor, offered apologies again for taking so much of the busy surgeon's time, offered some instructions on what to do about his effects, and soon died.

All other accounts Don read matched Colonel Doleman's version of Griswold having bled to death there on the Confederate side of the creek bank. There was no mention in any other book, pamphlet, or recollection about his being retrieved until after the shooting stopped, much less this stirring conversation between the dying captain and the faithful surgeon.

Then, in an excerpt from a Hartford-published pamphlet on the Connecticut regiments, Don found an account of the death of Lieutenant Allbritten of East Preston, the last of the three Eleventh Connecticut officers to die at Burnside. A sergeant named Albert Randolph, also from East Preston, was there in the ravine and recalled what happened:

We were talking to him about gathering up our wounded and getting ready to go again toward that bridge. He was a brave lad, a man ahead of his years. He was on the verge of giving us his specific orders when that awful sound of a cannon shot pierced our air. I ducked my head as did the others and when I looked up the brave Lieutenant Allbritten was falling forward before us, his handsome face, his entire stately head gone— vanished to eternity with his breath of life itself. That rebel shell struck him in the center of his head, lo and behold to God, blowing it to the winds and to the heavens. I had never seen anything like it before and I hope I never do again.

Don saw long streams of red blood and hunks and pieces of hair and skin and blue uniform and skull and brains splatter to the winds. Then he saw the bloody stump of a man's neck as the rest of his headless body fell to the ground. . . .

He felt nausea in his throat and heat in his chest. He rose from the table and walked outside into the warm Pennsylvania sunshine.

He needed a break from the horrors of the Eleventh Connecticut.

But he couldn't turn it off. While walking down the paths and under the trees of the War College's tranquil campus, his mind raced with questions.

Could those Thaddeus Farm remains be those of one of the Eleventh's forty who was known to have died at Burnside, one of those whose names were on the gray monument?

He made a mental note to check if the bodies of those forty were buried somewhere. At the National Cemetery at Antietam? In a cemetery back in Connecticut? Were they all present and accounted for under a headstone somewhere?

But could somebody, for any reason, have switched some bodies around?

Speaking of reasons—obviously, if some Confederates tied up the man and shot him they had to have had a reason. What reason? Did the Confederates really go around executing prisoners?

If that, in fact, was what happened. But why would it matter about the body? Why throw the ID disk of another man in the grave? Where did that disk come from anyhow?

And, while we're at it, let's not forget the healed broken arm of the guy in the grave. Could that possibly be relevant to any of this?

Questions, only questions. Yes, but they helped him move his mind and imagination from a man's head being blown apart. . . .

Back at the library, he picked up where he left off, reading first a gruesome, moving excerpt from a diary of a corporal in the Eleventh who was sent to a field hospital to recuperate from a wound suffered at Newberne. A War College archivist had clipped a note on the front of the small, blue notebook that said the man, who was from East Preston, had survived the slaughter at Burnside Bridge, only to die in the final Antietam battle on the far left flank.

There are 105 of us in this place that had before been home to a family. Its three small floors were now covered with men sleeping only on bare wooden planks that were mostly dripping with blood and death. Our coats were our only covering, our prayers were our only comforting. There was little water, and only occasionally did we eat some cooked cornmeal. I felt less of my life was there as each day passed. I felt that I would soon go to my maker and make my peace. On several nights the sounds of my comrades screaming for peace made me wish it would come sooner. Dying men make the sounds of animals dying.

Don couldn't imagine what a dying animal sounded like. Exactly what kind of animal was he talking about anyhow? But those words and the description of that hospital lingered with him for a few minutes. He tried to imagine himself there, lying on a floor in that place. He could not.

His mind bounced back to wondering about that list of unaccounted-fors. The man in the grave was an officer. He was wearing an officer's uniform. Could an officer have been unaccounted for?

Colonel Doleman would know the answer to that off the top of his head. He'd know about execution-style killings, too.

On the drive back to Washington, Don would call the old man on his cell phone. It would be great after today just to talk to him again anyway.

The colonel would also know more about those hospitals. What awful places they must have been.

Now. Onward to something else on this table. Yes. Onward from the Eleventh Connecticut to the Twenty-third Massachusetts. That was the outfit of T. L. Flintson, the name on that disk found with the Burnside remains.

Again, after picking a few facts from one book or pamphlet after another, Don knew the Twenty-third mustered and trained at a Lynnfield, Massachusetts, tent camp before marching off to Salem, boarding ships, and sailing to Annapolis to join the war.

It was a history, both in time and place, that was remarkably similar to the Eleventh Connecticut's. The Twenty-third was put under the command of Burnside and eventually participated in the battle for Newberne, North Carolina.

So both the Twenty-third and the Eleventh were at Newberne!

Don read on. Maybe, just maybe, he was on to something.

From another of the large books: When Burnside went off with the Eleventh and other regiments to join the Army of the Potomac, the Twenty-third was one of the regiments he left behind in Newberne to perform "provost duty." After scanning a few more lines about that, Don concluded that provost duty was a dignified way of saying it was there as an occupation army. It ran the hospitals and the local government and courts, and it maintained order among the few local people who remained. The soldiers also did a lot of parading and eating and drinking. Said one account: "Let's not forget the performances of the regimental Glee Club."

Don wanted to toss that book across the room.

The Glee Club? How dare the Twenty-third live the good life in North Carolina while men like Kingsbury and Griswold and Allbritten were experiencing hell and horror in Maryland!

He knew it wasn't fair to think that way, but he couldn't help it.

After taking a few deep breaths, he lectured himself on the fact of irrelevance. None of that mattered now. The important thing was that the Eleventh Connecticut and the Twenty-third Massachusetts fought together during the battle for Newberne and for several more weeks in that area of North Carolina.

That meant there were plenty of opportunities for a man of the Eleventh to come into the possession of an ID disk of a man of the Twenty-third—a man named T. L. Flintson.

There was a particular entry in the Twenty-third's regimental history that provided a hint of how it might have happened: "29 July. The sick in hospitals belonging to regiments which Burnside had taken away to reinforce McClellan on the Peninsula were sent to their regiments in Virginia."

That brought to Don's calmer mind the excerpt he had just

read from the diary of a Corporal Campbell of the Eleventh Connecticut. He was the East Preston man who described life in a regimental hospital at Newberne and spoke of dying men making the sounds of dying animals.

East Preston. East Preston. So many were from East Preston. Is that relevant?

And thus Don added another question to the list.

Don waited until he was well outside Carlisle and comfortably cruising on the interstate before dialing Colonel Doleman on his cell phone.

He immediately noticed a marked lack of robustness in the colonel's voice and response. "Are you all right, sir?" he asked.

"Under the weather a bit is all," the colonel said flatly. "Whatever that really means. Do you know where that expression comes from? Why do we civilized people say we're 'under the weather' when we're feeling sick or down or otherwise not together? Do you happen to know the answer to that question, doctor?"

"No, sir, I do not. But I will find out."

"No need to do that. You are busy trying to find out a more important thing right now. I take it you do not yet know the identity of our man?"

Don said that was true. He recounted most of what he and Reg Womach were doing to identify "our man," leaving out the possibility—certainty, really—that the man in the ground had been tied up and shot. He would bring that up later.

Then he told the colonel that he had learned thirty men from the Eleventh Connecticut were unaccounted for when the war ended. How likely, he wanted to know, was it that any officer, whether in the Eleventh Connecticut or any other outfit, would end up with nobody knowing what happened to him?

"Most unlikely," answered the colonel. "Most of the Union officers came from the monied, political, educated, or professional military classes. Their people would probably not have rested until they accounted for their son or husband or whatever."

The colonel cautioned Don about getting too fixated on the Eleventh Connecticut. "Remember, please, that while I suggested the probability of your man being from that outfit, that must not be considered gospel. There was chaos and confusion on that battlefield that day, and there are just too many other possibilities. He could be from Massachusetts or New Hampshire or even from Mars, for that matter."

"I'm from the eliminator school of archeology, colonel," said Don.

"And what, pray tell, is that?"

"We go at it one possibility at a time, starting with the best one. Eliminate it before moving on to possibility number two . . . and so on."

"And so on," the colonel said. "Historians tend to work differently—the vacuum-cleaner school, I guess you'd call it. Sweep up everything in sight and then sort through it."

Don, impatient as always, decided to jump to the most difficult subject: the possibility of the Confederates executing prisoners.

With force, the colonel said: "It was, in fact, one of the bloodiest, most awful wars ever fought, sir, but it was between men of honor, not between barbarians. They were all killers, as all civilized men can be when brought to full passion by patriotism, self-defense, or anger, but there was a tone of civility to the killing. Why do you ask, doctor?"

"I was just wondering if it was possible that our man in the grave might have been captured and then killed by his captors. They were then afraid of being caught and punished, so they buried him—"

"Eliminate it from your possibilities, young Doctor Eliminator. There is absolutely no way such a thing could happen. Not at Antietam, not at any place during that war. There were battlefield massacres, and there was mistreatment of prisoners at prison camps. But there was not one incident of that kind of summary execution. Not one. They killed, but they did not execute."

Not that anybody ever heard about, thought Don to himself. "Consider it eliminated, colonel," he said into the phone. "Thank you."

Don went back to a less incendiary subject: the hospitals. "How awful must they have been, colonel?"

"They were almost as bad as dying—worse for some," said Doleman. "There was a shortage of everything except saws to remove body parts. I have read reports that taking a wounded man to some hospitals—both Union and Confederate—was like condemning him to a certain death. If not from his wounds, from the disease he would contract there. I am no expert on that, however, doctor. If you are interested, keep reading. Everything that happened in this Civil War of ours is written down somewhere. It was the last of our major wars where there was no unit censorship. All combatants of all ranks on both sides were free to write their thoughts and opinions and stories to anyone they wished, whether they be private or public. The challenge, the obsession, the lovely magic is in the hunt to find it. It does not matter if you are from the eliminator or the vacuum-cleaner school, you still have to work very hard."

Don agreed and then, on a personal note, advised the colonel *not* to work too hard and to take it easy.

"I am, Doctor Spaniel. I am, in fact, speaking to you at this moment from my bed, whence I have been seldom removed for several days."

"I hope I didn't wear you out the other day at Antietam, colonel," he said.

"That was already done by the excitement of my life long before you called about your soldier on the hill, young Doctor Spaniel," said the colonel.

I first put an eye on that stone bridge at daybreak through a small telescope, borrowed from Lieutenant Allbritten. There had been a soft drizzle, and now it was gone, and there was the bridge. I saw it from our position on high ground 250 yards away. It seemed so peaceful, so serene, so ready for a postal card or a painter of landscape scenes to capture for suitable hanging on a New Haven parlor wall.

That first sighting was a lasting memory that came back afterward when I considered how that small gray structure caused so many people, including myself and my dear comrades in arms, to make so many ill-advised decisions that had as their result the taking of so many lives, limbs, and spirits. I mean not to philosophize, only to highlight truisms made real by experience.

I could also see the flowing creek called the Antietam that runs its course under the bridge. It, too, had a gentle appearance, a clear, silver sparkle that was soon to be discolored by the red of flowing blood from the veins of men in blue.

6

It was Saturday morning, the day after Carlisle. Don shot up out of bed with the rising sun and went right to his two large briefcases of Carlisle notes and papers on the desk in his living room.

But in a few minutes his head began to ache. Nothing of a migraine scale, but there was enough pain to send him a message: Take a break, Don. Or, in Reg's words: Get a grip, Don.

A book. Read a book. He had a new one on Heinrich Schliemann's famous archeological digs at Troy and another on the never-ending search in Ethiopia for the real beginnings of mankind. And then there was Ernest Furgurson's new Civil War chronicle of the battle of Richmond. . . .

No. He didn't feel like reading anything—not Furgurson, not even a magazine, including the new issue of *Archaeology Today*, which had just arrived with fresh photos of an Indian-mound site in Kentucky.

He needed a *real* distraction, something to stop him from thinking about that man who died 134 years ago on the high ground overlooking a bridge across a creek called the Antietam.

So he did what he had not done since he was about nine years old. He turned on the set to watch Saturday-morning television.

He was a surfer. He didn't watch television much even at night, but when he did he could not resist the lure of the remote control. He usually zipped from channel to channel with lightning speed, hearing only a few words and seeing only a glimpse of a scene or a person from each of the forty-two channels available from his northern Virginia cable system.

Now he heard the voice of Barney and then that of a senator in a C-SPAN repeat of a floor debate about a Haiti resolution. Click. The secretary of the navy testifying before a congressional committee about base closings. Click. A Headline News report from a war zone that was very cold. A two-month-old trial on Court TV of an old man's claim in a California municipal court against a hearing aid company. Click.

Two men wrestling. Wrestling in the morning? One of the wrestlers was called the British Bulldog. His shorts were a print of the British flag. His opponent, a man with hair down to his waist, was the Heartbreak Kid. Click.

He lingered for a count of ten at a shoot-out between two thuggy men in a vast warehouse. It was a cop movie on the Encore Channel. Click. *Care Bears* on Disney. Click. *Spiderman* on Fox. *Bump in the Night* on ABC, *Garfield and Friends* on CBS, *Frugal Gourmet* on PBS. Click, click, click.

He was halfway through the entire selection of channels for the fifth time when something important began to happen.

The Virginia state high school wrestling championships on a local public-broadcasting station. The final match in the 160-pound class. A kid named Allred versus a kid named Castro. Allred was ahead by five points.

Click. Click.

The two pro wrestlers, the British Bulldog and the Heartbreak Kid, were still at it on USA. . . .

Wrestling.

Who watches or cares about wrestling?

Wrestling. Wrestling! *Wrestling!*

Reg had said, Find a Burnside dead man who had fallen out of a tree or been a wrestler. . . .

Don now remembered reading about wrestling somewhere in something at Carlisle. Was it in an account concerning one of those Eleventh Connecticut officers who died at Burnside? He had wrestled in college? At West Point? No, no. But there was something.

Which officer was it? Kingsbury? Griswold? Allbritten?

Don leaped back to the desk.

He couldn't find it in any of his notes. Also, none of the straight bios of Kingsbury and Griswold of Lyme and Allbritten of East Preston made any reference to wrestling. They dealt mostly with the three men's families, education, and military backgrounds. There was nothing about athletics.

Where had he seen a mention of wrestling? There had been wrestling in the world since ancient times, so it was certainly around during the time of the Civil War.

Maybe it wasn't a direct reference he had read. Maybe it was something that triggered another thought that led to still another. . . .

He went through his photocopies and notes from Carlisle again.

Maybe he really was sick. The headache was a symptom of delusions, brought on by his Antietam obsession. It had been aggravated by watching snippets of the British Bulldog and the Heartbreak Kid.

He found something. A few sentences in the pages copied from the big 1868 Connecticut history book. It was the account of an evening encampment before the battle of South Mountain. He had read the sentences yesterday at Carlisle. They had meant nothing then.

A young corporal in the Eleventh Connecticut had written to his mother back in East Preston—there it was again: "The night, dear mother, is filled with the sweet smells of burning hardwood and roasting yellow corn. There are sounds of laughter and of singing and storytelling coming from all directions. I must stop writing soon to join the others in watching one of our officers demonstrate the art of personal combat. He is said to be most skilled in throwing men about, even those who outweigh him by many pounds."

Wrestling, in other words.

Click.

Who was the officer?

Within minutes, he had an answer. He found a few crucial sentences that pointed right at the identity of the officer/wrestler—and thus the man in the grave. They were from a story in the September 29, 1862, edition of the weekly newspaper in East Preston, Connecticut, a copy of which was in the stack of copied material he had brought back from Carlisle. It was an account of a funeral that he had only glanced at before.

Lieutenant Allbritten was known by his friends for his intelligence, his courage and bravery, his sweet disposition, his devotion to church and family, and his special talents in the sport of wrestling. The walls in our town will reverberate forever with the tales of his courage and strength on the mats and floors of Connecticut as well as the battlefields of North Carolina, Virginia, and Maryland. His young widow and infant son will be able to cherish that legacy of their fallen husband and father, too.

Click.

Kenneth L. Allbritten, lieutenant, Eleventh Connecticut Volunteers. The officer who died after Kingsbury and Griswold. The one who died a terrible death in that ravine!

The one whose head was blown away. Or so it was said.

Don was about to reach for the phone to call Reg, to say, with some pride, that the broken arm had turned out to be a terrific clue.

But he read on. The story in the East Preston *Record* was about Kenneth Allbritten's burial as well as a funeral.

"The remains of the fallen hero of Antietam, America's bloodiest day in history, were laid to rest next to those of his grandfather and grandmother, who were among the settlers and leaders of East Preston and of our way of life."

So. There were remains somebody had claimed were those of Kenneth L. Allbritten, lieutenant, Eleventh Connecticut Volunteers, in a cemetery in a small town in Connecticut.

And there was another set of bones lain out on a table on the fourth floor of the Natural History Museum in Washington, D.C., that also appeared to be those of Lieutenant Allbritten.

Then Don read some really bad news. It was in the last sentence of that September 29, 1862, newspaper story.

It read: "There was no viewing of Lieutenant Allbritten as is the custom in his Christian faith because of the nature of his mortal wound."

That could mean Kenneth L. Allbritten's head was blown away.

Don's spirits, lifted by the wrestling revelation, crashed back down. *If there are headless remains in an East Preston, Connecticut, grave, then, obviously, that skeleton on Reg's lab table cannot be Allbritten's.*

So much for the *Click!* about wrestling. And, as with the earlier ID disk episode, welcome to another beginning.

Maybe a place to start this time would be East Preston, Connecticut?

Our formal orders that morning came from our magnificent commanding officer, Colonel Henry W. Kingsbury. His words of command and inspiration were delivered to us by Kenneth Allbritten, our beloved lieutenant and friend.

" 'The time has come for us to demonstrate to our adversaries on this field before us, this field of battle, as well as to the leaders of our Union here and elsewhere, to our loved and cherished ones in our homes and hearts, what we are made of physically, patriotically, and spiritually,' " Lieutenant Allbritten recited.

He read the words of the colonel from a piece of wrinkled paper that he held in his two hands in front of him, only slightly higher than his waist. His hands were, like his voice, aquiver like poplar limbs in the wind. His speaking style, always a mite unsteady and high in pitch in normal discourse, was at the peak of its scale and tremble. These were most anxious times, and it was understandable this would have such an effect.

" 'Our mission this morning, dear brave soldiers of Connecticut, is to charge and seize a little bridge over a narrow creek called the Antietam. We will accomplish this feat by forming a skirmish line and, on order, rushing to our goal at quick-time, with full honor and valor.' "

I noted the change in Kenneth Allbritten's eyes when he looked up and around at us, his friends from East Preston, his comrades in arms. His eyes had always been such a flowing and glowing blue, but this morning that blue was encircled with large loops of red. Had the nightmares of what might lie ahead driven him to fits of awakened anxiety and concern for his men and mission? This was an inquiry to be made only in the deepest privacy of my mind.

Also on the matter of appearance, Kenneth Allbritten's blue tunic and uniform trousers of a proud officer of the Union were as wrinkled and wet from a light early morning rain as were mine and those of my fellow soldiers in the enlisted ranks. I had attempted mightily to have myself and the good men under my command look their best for this day of destiny and decision, but the elements of the morning, taken with the many recent days of difficult marching and camping that preceded, made such a goal an impossible dream. None of us had put a moment's effort toward trimming our chin whiskers in weeks. We would have to make up in courage and determination what we lacked in creases and neatness in our personal appearance, our military bearing.

" 'At the bridge, we will be joined from our right flank by a brigade of brave soldiers from the great state of Ohio and, together, we will cross the bridge in triumph, watching the defeated rears of the Confederates scatter like scared chickens in a vain search for sanctuary from certain defeat and annihilation.' "

The passing of time was something impossible to calculate, but it seemed as if it were only a matter of scant seconds before we heard the words of engagement:

"Forward! Onward! Double-quick!"

Lieutenant Allbritten, together with Captain John Griswold, another man of bravery and example, led us at quick-step over a small hill, down through a slight drop in the land, and then up and over another rise. The creek and the bridge were then visible and, it appeared to the eye, in close, easy grasp.

Oh, dear God, what a miscalculation!

We were hit with an onslaught of fire and noise that is beyond my abilities to describe. My ears were assaulted by a pounding boom from cannon and rifle fire that I was sure would cause them to pour blood. My eyes and nostrils were full of acrid smoke. I could see nothing directly before me except a scene of hell—of men sprawling and falling and rolling.

I felt something wet on my right arm. Rain? Had the rain returned? The wet was red. . . .

There by my side before my unbelieving eyes was a bleeding man, his face beyond recognition for a name, sinking down on his knees. The lower portion of his jaw had been carried away, and the torn fragments that remained, together with his tongue, clotted with gore, hung down upon his breast.

I felt that all the demons of hell had been turned loose—all the dogs of war unleashed to rend us into shreds. There were long volleys of musketry vomiting their furious discharges of pestilential lead. The atmosphere was crowded by the exploding shells, baleful fires gleamed through the foliage across the creek, as if myriads of fireflies were flitting through the boughs, and there was a fringe of vivid, sparking flame spurting out along the skirt of the forest above and before us, while the concussion of the cannon seemed to make the hills tremble and totter.

I could hear discordant, disconnected shouts above the roar.

"Onward! Over here! Over there! Take cover!"

I kept running forward. We were in an open field. I looked up to my left, across the creek at that concert of flashes from weapons firing from trees and from behind barriers. Their brutally hot and deadly force was striking men around me as we ran, as we sought scant refuge behind a frail rail fence and sapling trees.

Nothing in my training or in my imagination had equipped me as a human being or as a soldier to bear witness to the horror that was all around me. My eyes and ears and other senses ran over with death and hurt.

I heard the smash and crack and sizzle of shells against bodies, the smashing of bones. I heard the screaming from the mouths and the souls of young men of Connecticut.

"Help! Help me! Save me! God! Help me!"

For some, there was no saving possible. I dropped down next to such a man. One of the enemy's shells had plowed a groove in the skull of the fellow and had cut his face downward—a dreadful spectacle.

I rose again to the sound of another man cursing a comrade for lying on him heavily. He was cursing a dying man.

We had been made easy targets for the Confederate soldiers, who were able to shoot down at us from behind good concealment, cover, and protection. They essentially picked us off at will. I must say, even now as I write these words for another purpose, my hand cannot help but shake with anger. Let me say most directly that no armed men, Americans of any kind or persuasion or men of any other nation, should ever be put in such an exposed position without there being consequences for the commanders who do so.

Please excuse the fury. It will always be with me.

I was almost to the water of the creek when I heard shouts of "Withdraw! To the high ground! Withdraw! To the trees! Withdraw!"

I turned and ran as fast as I could in the direction from which we had come. There were the fallen bodies of men in blue to my right, to my left, to my front. I had to swivel my hips and leap with care in order to avoid stepping on them and the messes of their death and suffering.

The smell filling my nostrils suddenly was no longer that of muskets and cannons and burned powder. It was that of blood and other fluids of the body and that of burning skin and muscles, fingers and toes, arms and legs, backs and stomachs, eyes and hair.

Not all of the bodies were lifeless. I halted my hasty withdrawal to grab up a man with no left leg below the knee, it having been blown off and away, most probably by a direct hit from a Reb cannon. I recognized him. He was Elmer Whitfield of Ridgewood, and he was screaming for help or death, for salvation or termination. I grabbed him by his shoulders, clamped his left arm around my neck, and assisted his one-leg hop up the incline to the trees and the high ground where there would be a respite, a place for him to cry and die in peace, if nothing more. I felt the stump of his left leg bumping incessantly against me as we moved slowly toward safety.

We of the Eleventh Connecticut, the men whom all supposed could easily seize that little bridge over that narrow creek, had been splattered like hunted game and scattered like so many chickens.

Don began Monday, the first workday after his return to square one, with a taste of hardtack. He had gone to the kitchen and, as always, to his small stainless-steel bread box to begin the preparation of his breakfast. But, instead of grabbing the usual English muffin or piece of bread to toast, he came up with a piece of that hardtack Henry Milliken had given him. With little thought, he had tossed the package in the bread box when he had returned from Sharpsburg several days ago.

Now, also with little thought, he undid the cellophane wrapping around the stack of ten crackers. The outside box—from G. H. Bent Co. of Milton, Massachusetts—said these crackers for Civil War reenactor soldiers were exactly like those the company had made for the real ones. There was a hungry soldier's plea quoted on the box that Don had read before, about these things that were often eaten despite being bug or crud infested.

> *It is the dying wail of the starving.*
> *Hard crackers, hard crackers,*
> *come again once more.*
> *You were old and very wormy,*
> *but we pass your failings o'er.*
> *O hard crackers, come again,*
> *come again once more.*

The cracker, about a half-inch thick, was perforated by a dozen or so holes, each the size of a small nail. Don bit into the cracker. His teeth didn't go through. It was as hard as a block of wood. He held the cracker in his mouth, between his teeth, until his saliva had moistened it enough for him to bite down. The taste was saltless, dry, arid, rocky. No wonder, thought Don, that Civil War soldiers sought always to dunk hardtack in coffee, soup, even water before putting it in their mouths.

Then, at the office a short time later, Reg called.

"Wilkins, the FBI firearms guy, has something he says is most interesting," said Reg.

"I need something interesting, that's for sure," said Don. And he told Reg about the other set of remains in Connecticut—and, in passing, his ups and downs about wrestling.

"Hey, Don, you should have known that wrestling thing was a throwaway line—not a serious clue," Reg said. "A lot of American males over twelve have had at least one broken arm."

Please don't tell me what I should have known, Don thought, but did not say. He said nothing.

Reg tried to cheer him up. "You're going to sort it out. I know you will."

"I think we should go to East Preston, Connecticut—that's Allbritten's hometown, where he's buried."

"What are we going to do, dig up his grave?"

"I don't know what I'm going to do," Don said. "I just have a feeling we might find something."

"Sure, fine," Reg said. "Meantime, Wilkins says to come to his lab on the fourth floor of the FBI building—"

"I'm on my way. I'll meet you there?"

"No way. She'd kill me instead of just leaving me if she saw me now."

True, thought Don. Reg and Susan, the hair expert, had had an ongoing problem about the length of his hair. Susan, claiming hair spoke to her the way bones did to Reg, said she didn't like the message of a general personality and character slovenliness coming from his. Reg told Don she had had a full-blown screaming fit the morning he first put his hair in a ponytail with a rubber band. He had had his hair cut immediately and kept it mostly short from then on. But now, eight months after their split-up, it was longer than it had ever been.

Don seldom spoke to Reg or anyone else about his own love life, mostly because there wasn't much of interest to talk about. He had come close to marriage more than once, the last time involving an antitrust lawyer who worked on the Microsoft case for the Justice Department. She seemed to speak for most of the women who had come and gone from Don's life when she announced—loudly over dinner at a Georgetown restaurant—that she didn't wish to share her life with America's only civil war. Don figured that someday he would meet somebody who didn't mind. Maybe Faye Lee Sutton? There was no rush.

He did rush to the FBI building to see what Bob Wilkins had to show him.

Wilkins, a taciturn man in his late thirties, motioned for Don to look through the double-view aperture of a comparison microscope—"the scope," he called it.

"The bullet on the left is the control. That is what we know for a fact to be a slug that was fired from a particular make and model of firearm. That piece on the right is that fragment Womach sent over to me. Do you see the similarities? I have set the scope so they are at the identical spot on both."

The fragment was covered with a patina of white oxide and was scarred. But, yes, Don could see some similarities.

"Right, I see them," he said.

Wilkins said: "The deterioration through the years has removed many of the specific markings and characteristics that would make it possible to pinpoint the exact weapon. The only certainty I can give you is for the manufacturer and the model, not the specific weapon. It wouldn't work in a murder case today, but it might help you-all."

Clearly Wilkins, like Reg and most every one of these scientist specialists, had a need to dispense his information and findings in lecture form. This FBI guy was talking to Don in a loud, deliberate way that was more suitable for a classroom of recruits at the FBI Academy.

At least Wilkins had gotten right down to business and hadn't started, for instance, with a lesson on the scope, the most important tool there is to anyone involved in ballistics or firearms investigation. Don already knew how two separate microscope tubes were used so that separate slides or objects could be looked at simultaneously—and comparatively—through the use of various prisms.

Wilkins continued: "The land-and-groove markings are the keys to all. Particularly on this one. They're about all we can read from that fragment you gave me. But it's a pretty good read. Look carefully at the way they twist in both."

Don looked.

Then he went with Wilkins into a small conference room off one corner of the laboratory. Wilkins gave Don a cup of coffee and a piece of paper.

"I've put it all in writing so you'll have it," said Wilkins. "But what we have here is a positive ID on your fragment. The left-hand twist land-and-groove markings clearly identified it as fired from a Colt revolver. There are six lands and grooves, as in a few particular models of Colt revolvers. That slug on the left is from our master file. We know for a fact that it was fired from a specific model of Colt revolver—the 1860 Police Revolver. Only a few were made, none was issued to Union officers, but many of them bought them on their own for twenty dollars apiece. . . . What's the matter, Doctor Spaniel? You look like you've seen a ghost."

Don said: "That was the kind of pistol that was found in our man's grave. That was his side-arm. A Colt 1860 Police Revolver. I have it back at my office. It's the same pistol."

Wilkins said: "Like I said earlier, there's not enough in the fragment to determine what exact 1860 Police Colt it came from. Can the one you found be fired?"

"No, no, it's all rusted—none of the parts still move," Spaniel said. "Did the Confederates use Police Colts?"

"Not that I have ever heard. It's most unlikely."

"But isn't it possible for a Confederate to have taken one from a prisoner or found one on a battlefield?"

"Sure. But could we be talking suicide by your guy in the ground?" asked Wilkins.

"Not unless he was some kind of carnival contortionist capable of holding a pistol behind him in such a way as to fire a shot up through the base of his skull from the rear," said Don. "And with his hands tied together behind his back."

"I feel I may have thickened your plot and situation a bit," Wilkins said.

Don agreed that he had indeed done that.

He had also given Don another very good reason to go to East Preston, Connecticut.

Colonel Kingsbury was among the wounded. I did not see the fallen hero, but we heard from those who did that he appeared in a condition that forecast a sure and quick death from his wounds. A corporal from New Haven who had been with the colonel bore witness to the most unsurprising fact that, despite his wrenching injuries, the great man never stopped leading by example, never ceased rallying the troops around him to rise beyond the awfulness of the occasion, to persevere, to prevail—to show one and all of what they were made. I wondered, but never determined, if one of those voices of exhortation I had heard from out there in the burning, smoky chaos a few minutes before belonged to Colonel Kingsbury.

Again, there being no frame of mind or device for keeping an accurate click-click-click record of time, it seemed like only hairs of seconds before someone shouted to get ready for a second charge at the bridge.

My immediate thought was that such a thing bordered on madness, but I quickly saw that the words of rally were coming from Captain Griswold. I jumped to my feet and yelled at soldiers around me to be up and ready.

Again, we formed a skirmish line and moved out at quick-step. Again, within seconds after leaving the haven of the trees and the high ground, we were hit by showers of lead and destruction. Captain Griswold, clearly frustrated and turned to hero by the situation of Colonel Kingsbury's martyrdom, raced in front of us toward the creek.

"We will get the Reb! We will get the Reb! Follow me! Follow me!" were the words he used to summon our bodies and our courage to follow him.

Several of us, through what I considered to be pure miracle, most likely with the direct intervention of the Almighty Himself, made it to the bank of the creek right behind the captain. I watched with stunning fascination as Captain Griswold raised his right hand high over his head and waved it furiously toward the bank on the other side.

"Follow me!" he shouted. "Into the water! Follow me!"

He stepped down and into the creek! I was right behind him. A few others—I could not count heads at that moment—joined us. The water, flowing smoothly as if nothing unusual were happening in and around it, felt cold, soothing, comforting. After two steps, the water level was up to my chest. I could see the captain in front of me some five or six yards and the ground of the bank on the other side. I calculated that it would take only a few minutes to get there. I had just begun to calculate what we, a mere handful of wet Union soldiers, might do against the defending Confederate force of snipers and cannon on the other side, when I bore witness to a horror that remains in my sight to this day, ten years later, with the permanence of a lithograph print, a painting in oils, a statue of granite.

A careening, whining Reb shot struck Captain Griswold in the chest, spewing a spray of blood and blue uniform and brass buttons and hairy skin and cracked bones into the sky. He turned back. On this man's once tranquil face, there was a grimace of a silent shriek unlike any I have ever before witnessed. He waved to me to go back, go back. I remained steady—almost as if frozen in that moving water of that creek. Right before me, as if someone had emptied a bottle of dye into the water, it became red from the blood of my young captain.

I turned around, away from him, back toward the creek bank from where I had come. So did the others. I could see now that there were only five of us—only five out of however many who had followed our captain's lead. With each hurried step I took in the water came an expectation, a certainty, that I would be hit from behind by a shot of lead similar to the one that had struck Captain Griswold.

I arrived at the shore, another miracle to me, still unstruck and alive, and pulled myself onto the ground. Lying down in order to make myself as small and obscure a target to Reb snipers as possible, I witnessed the captain's final steps in the water, then at the far bank, where he managed with a martyr's superhuman strength to pull himself onto ground and to lie facedown on that ground, his arms and hands stretched out before him.

I ached to enter the water again, wade to the other side, and retrieve our captain's body. But others said such a mission would be certain to end in failure. My guilt over having not accompanied my leader through the water to the other side haunted my soul and spirit then and continues to do so now. My life is one lived only with the haunts of that day at the Antietam.

I have sought to remember the exact moment that I, Albert Randolph, came to the stark realization that my death while in the service of the Eleventh Connecticut Volunteer Regiment was no longer an issue of mere possibility. Rather, it was clearly an inevitability, an event as sure to come as the sunshine on a golden Indian-summer day in my beloved western Connecticut. That moment was there on that Maryland creek bank, watching as a coward while a brave man bled to death onto the ground across a narrow creek. I not only believed death to be only one minié ball, one exploding shell, one bayonet stab away, I also believed it to be coming as a welcome blessing. Kill me if you must, Reb, kill me as you must.

7

They parked at the cemetery behind the Zion Episcopal Church a few minutes before ten o'clock. It was a small cemetery, the final resting place for a few hundred departed citizens of East Preston, Connecticut. The city-limits sign said East Preston had a population of 2,570 and had been founded in 1758. This cemetery had the magnificent look and feel and silence of a place that had been there from the beginning.

Don and Reg had driven into the town from the north, so it wasn't until they had parked that they saw that the cemetery and the church were on a narrow street on the north side of the town green. It was a rectangle, two thirds the size of a football field, that was outlined by streets with several one- and two-story buildings on the other three sides.

Don Spaniel's and Reg Womach's lines of work made them at home in cemeteries. But it was not the familiarity that preachers or funeral directors might have. Don's and Reg's emotions were mixed with a restlessness. Don could not help thinking that what lay under those headstones were real people with stories to tell about their lives and times. Reg had said to Don that after reading a death date on a tombstone he immediately wondered what state of decomposition the remains might be in and what mysteries they might reveal.

Neither wanted to go around digging up graveyards, but both welcomed it when some act of nature, such as a flood, or even of commerce, such as a new shopping center, gave them the opportunity.

Seldom had they wished for a flood or a shopping center more than they did now, at this moment in East Preston, Connecticut.

There it was. There *he* was.

A gray granite block, similar in size and majesty to the Eleventh Connecticut's at Burnside Bridge.

Mounted on it was a four-foot-high statue of a smooth-faced young man in a Union officer's uniform. The inscription was made in Old English style.

Kenneth Leonard Allbritten
Lieutenant, Eleventh Connecticut Volunteers
Born, April 12, 1841
Died, September 17, 1862.
This young hero of East Preston, this brave man of God,
was struck down by an enemy cannon shot on that battlefield
of hell called Antietam.

———

Oh, rare and royal was the sacrifice!
For you and me they put their armor on;
For you and me they stood in grim array
Where death came hurtling; and for you and me
They joined the mortal struggle, and went down
Amid the mad, tumultuous whirl of flame.

W. A. Croffut

Don recognized the author of those lines. Croffut was the coauthor of that big 1868 book on Connecticut's history in the Civil War.

Reg read aloud the sentence: " 'This young hero of East Preston, this brave man of God, was struck down by an enemy cannon shot on that battlefield of hell called Antietam.' "

They said nothing else to each other for several minutes.

They had managed to come here this morning because an airline price war had broken out on the one-hour-fifteen-minute flight from Washington-Dulles to Hartford, Connecticut. As a result, neither Don nor Reg had any trouble getting supervisor approval for the trip—up and back on the same day.

"Well, whatever this inscription says, he may not be the one down there, right?" Reg said finally. "Let's find out. Did you bring your archeologist's trowel, doctor?"

Reg had made no secret of his belief that, short of digging up Allbritten's grave, this trip to East Preston was unlikely to produce much of anything. Don knew he was being humored, but he didn't mind, particularly after Reg had said—just to give it some purpose for him—that he might look for a photograph of Kenneth Allbritten. He said there was a new technique using computers, skulls, and photographs that could sometimes help identify remains.

That sounded great to Don, the vacuum cleaner. He had come to sweep through everything he could find. His only specific quest was for information about a particular pistol.

There was a larger statue of a Union soldier just a few yards away on the town green. But this one was that of an enlisted man, not an officer.

The words on the pedestal were different, too: "In memory of those beloved men of East Preston who gave the ultimate sacrifice to preserve the sacred union of the United States of America in the war of 1861–1865."

There were seven names listed underneath: Allbritten's and six others.

Don wrote down the other six.

A few yards away, they came across a thin granite marker that rose out of the ground a yard high. Its words, written vertically on one side: "Site of Recruiting Tent for Eleventh Connecticut Vol. Inf'y.—August 1861."

"If they had known what was coming at that bridge across the Antietam, they might not have gone into that tent," said Reg.

"I'm not so sure," said Don. He remembered that Colonel Doleman believed the fear of death seemed almost totally absent from the young men who fought on both sides of the Civil War.

Don and Reg started across to the other side of the green, a truly magnificent expanse of golf-course grass, old brick sidewalks, and weedless beds of yellow and white daffodils. Don, recalling East Preston's 1758 founding date, had no trouble imagining portly men in breeches and long coats and beards playing roll pins and smoking long pipes and talking about the Tea Tax, the coming of the British, and other affairs of colonial America.

They were looking for a small, one-story, brown brick building on the green with a sign in front that said: EAST PRESTON HISTORICAL SOCIETY AND MUSEUM. A member of Don's research staff had come up with those directions after first identifying the place's existence and what they hoped would be helpful contents.

They saw the building almost immediately, but Reg had seen something else, too. He stopped Don. "Look over there," he said, nodding toward a different building. It was a two-story structure that clearly had been a bank or something else substantial many years before. On the ground level was a café called The Place on the Green.

Then Don saw what Reg was really pointing out: ALLBRITTEN implanted in ornate concrete up near the top of the building.

Reg motioned again in another direction. "And over there, too."

The green-and-white-crossed street sign at the intersection said Mackenzie going north and south and Allbritten running east and west.

They went to the historical society, which was next to a much larger white frame building that had a sign on it that declared it to be TOWN HALL.

Walking inside the history building, Don was immediately struck by how perfect a place it was for its function. It had the dust and powdery ambience of something that might have been around itself since 1758. So did the woman who greeted them.

She was at least seventy-five years old and was as friendly and helpful as it was possible to be without jeopardizing her perfect New England Yankee reserve. She asked no questions about who they might be or why they were interested in the town of East Preston during the time of the Civil War. She was there to see to the needs of anyone who walked in, and that was what she did.

She invited Don to look at a three-foot-square glass display case of Civil War soldiers' artifacts. It had some uniform buttons, several unspent bullets, and two ID disks, as well as a pair of boots, an enlisted man's blue kepi, and other items that, according to a small handwritten card, had been carried by East Preston soldiers serving in the Eleventh Connecticut Volunteer Regiment. She also said he should feel free to look at anything on the shelves next to the case in a section labeled "Civil War." There were several long shelves, each filled with written and other paper material.

Following Reg's request to see any Civil War–era photographs in the society's collection, the woman escorted him to a tiny room in the back. "All of our photos are arranged in boxes by years—at least, they're supposed to be," she said. "Just help yourself."

Using a library table, smaller but not unlike the one he had at Carlisle, Don started going through the paper material. There were personnel rosters, photocopies of soldier diaries and letters, official proclamations, and bound copies of the East Preston *Record*, including the edition that contained the Allbritten wrestling reference.

Don soon found several other wrestling mentions concerning Allbritten. He was clearly well-known and well-admired for his abilities to throw and pin other men in competitions at college and local fairs.

But there was nothing—not yet—about the type of pistol Lieutenant Allbritten took to war.

Don moved to collecting basic information about the East Preston men who fought in the Civil War, some of which he wrote down in a small spiral-bound notebook. For a few items, he paid the nice lady fifteen cents a page to make copies on a machine in the back, where Don would not have been surprised to hear the voices of the East Preston gentry debating whether to send their sons off to fight the Confederates or, even earlier, to fight for independence from Britain.

The information he collected included the fact that Kenneth Leonard Allbritten was one of ten from the town who joined the Eleventh Connecticut Volunteers. A graduate of Yale, Allbritten was the only officer. He signed up first in Hartford and then returned to East Preston and helped recruit the others, many of whom he had known since childhood.

Don tried to imagine the scene in a tent back there on the green. Did Allbritten sit behind a table and give each man a pitch and then a piece of paper to sign? What did he say? What did he tell them it would be like to serve with him in the Union army? Did the potential recruits ask a lot of questions before signing on the dotted line? Did any of them say no thanks and walk out?

Three of the ten who did volunteer, according to what Don found and recorded, were wounded in the battle of Newberne. One of them recovered quickly and rejoined the Eleventh in time to fight at Antietam. That sounded familiar to Don.

Roland Mackenzie was one of only two who survived Antietam and the entire war and returned to East Preston. The other was a sergeant named Randolph, whose name Don had read before. Hadn't he come up somewhere in his Carlisle reading?

Don drew a harsh line in his notebook under the name of Randolph, whose first name was Albert. Albert Randolph. Don remembered. He was the one who wrote the vivid description of Allbritten's horrible death—a description that, at Carlisle, had, along with the Gardner photographs, overwhelmed Don's imagination.

He searched the shelf material for any other eyewitness accounts of Allbritten's death. He finally found one in a newspaper obituary of Roland Mackenzie, the other Eleventh Connecticut survivor—the Mackenzie, no doubt, whose name was on that street sign perpendicular to Allbritten. Mackenzie died at the age of eighty-one after a successful postwar career as a banker and civic leader in East Preston. He even served six years as the mayor of the town. Then, way down in the story, Don found what he was looking for.

Mr. Mackenzie was one of the brave soldiers from East Preston who was present at the battle of Antietam when Lieutenant Kenneth L. Allbritten was mortally wounded by a rebel cannon shot.

Mr. Mackenzie often described that scene as horror beyond description. He said the head of Lieutenant Allbritten was destroyed by the shot. Mr. Mackenzie said everyone in East Preston should pay tribute to the heroism of their son, Kenneth Leonard Allbritten.

Fine. But what kind of pistol did he have?

Meanwhile, Don looked through everything for an obituary of Albert Randolph. He could find none. *What happened to you, Albert Randolph?*

"Time for a break." Reg was standing at the table in front of Don. They had been at work for barely an hour, and Don was anxious to keep at it. But there was a grin on Reg's face that said, It's *really* time for a break.

They told the lady in charge that they would return shortly to resume their research and politely excused themselves.

Reg waited until they were seated at a table at The Place on the Green and had ordered coffees.

"I got it," he said, removing something from an inside pocket of his suit coat. "Look at this."

It was a photocopy of a photograph. Don took it in his hands. It was a standard Civil War portrait of a somber young man in a Union officer's uniform.

"This is our man?" he said softly to Reg.

"Yes, sir," Reg whispered back. "Lieutenant Kenneth L. Allbritten. Taken by a photographer in Hartford two weeks before the regiment left for New York and points south."

Don put the photo right up to his face, turned it over, back again, stared at it.

"I paid our little lady friend fifteen cents to make that copy."

Don said, "Tell me again what you might be able to do with this."

Reg, quietly, with the tone of a teacher dealing with a slow learner, again explained—he had already gone through it on the plane—an identification technique developed by a Smithsonian colleague and the FBI. Using computers and video cameras, they could compare a found skull with a predeath photograph of somebody and come reasonably close to determining a match.

"You really think you could prove for sure that skull back in your lab is the skull underneath that face in this picture?" Don asked.

"I don't know—but it's worth a try," Reg said. "And for the record, it's not just streets that are named for Allbritten and Mackenzie. Who was Mackenzie, by the way?"

Don told him about Mackenzie, one of two Antietam survivors from East Preston.

"Well, I saw photographs of all sizes and ages of most everything in town. Both the library and an elementary school are named for Allbritten. The middle school has Mackenzie's name on it, and so does a state park somewhere outside town."

Don couldn't keep his eyes off the photograph of Kenneth L. Allbritten. "He looks so innocent and strong, doesn't he?" he said. The strength was in his broad shoulders and thick neck. The innocence came from his curly dark hair, full mustache, sparkling eyes, and fresh face.

"Based on the size of his skull—if that's his back in my lab— I'd bet he was smart, too," said Reg.

"The stories I just read about him said he was brilliant—top grades all through all schools," said Don. "I wish you could tell from a photograph whether somebody broke his arm while wrestling."

"I told you—forget that one, Don."

"It's hard to imagine him with that head blown away."

Don took one last long look at the face of Allbritten. "What if we find out he or Mackenzie or somebody else wasn't a real hero after all? What if as a result they want to change the names of streets and buildings and other things?"

"Those are questions only gods and politicians can answer, doctor," Reg said. "And we ain't either of those."

They finished their coffee and agreed to go back to their labors for a couple of hours or so. Reg clearly was ready to go on back to Washington with his Allbritten picture, but he told Don he could keep himself occupied looking through more boxes of photographs. He loved old photographs.

Forget that, Don said, and suggested that Reg lend him a hand at the shelves and table.

"I still have to find out about that pistol," he said. "But I also want to know what became of a man named Albert Randolph."

For more than an hour, they read through newspapers and every scrap of material available. Neither came across even a passing mention of the pistol or Randolph.

Don decided to ask the little old lady for some assistance. He went over to her desk, grinned, bowed slightly, and said, "Pardon me, ma'am, but I'm trying to find out what happened to a man named Albert Randolph. He was from East Preston and fought with the Eleventh Connecticut in the Civil War."

She showed a flicker of interest. But she said nothing. So he continued. "From everything I have been able to determine, he survived the war and returned to East Preston. But there is no record, at least none that we can find, that shows what happened to him afterward."

She looked off and up to her right and repeated the name. "Albert Randolph."

She said it again as if the repetition might trigger a memory, a fact.

"I recall seeing something recently about a man with that last name. Randolph. I remember it because I had a nephew who met and married a young woman who had gone to a college somewhere in Virginia named Randolph-Macon. That was years ago. Yes. But the thought, the memory was within the last few weeks—or months. What was I looking at when I saw that name Randolph? Let me think. Randolph. Randolph. The word is familiar because I have seen it recently. Now where was that . . ."

She did not finish her sentence. Instead, she reached into a drawer in her desk. She pulled out a file folder and opened it. It was filled with letters, attached to their envelopes with paper clips.

"We're not good about answering our mail here because we simply do not have the time and the resources," she said. "But we read our mail. We read everything that is sent to us. That's more than most people do, isn't it?"

Don agreed that was more than most people do. One of the most famous archeologists in Britain was known within the profession for taking as many as seven years to respond to even simple inquiries. He was constantly in jeopardy of having his London flat repossessed, his water and lights turned off, his grandchildren think him dead.

She began looking through the stack of letters. It was three inches high. "Let me see if I can put my hands on that particular letter. It was from somebody out in the west, if I recall. Somebody with a question of some kind. I hope I have remembered correctly, and I hope I can find it."

Don said: "What if we gave you a hand with those letters? Three pairs of hands on the pump make for triple the water pumped."

She smiled and handed him more than half the letters.

Reg joined him at the desk. Each skimmed through his stack as fast as he could. They were looking only for the name Randolph.

Don found it after a few minutes.

The two-year-old letter was from a woman, probably also seventy-five years old, who ran the Marion County Historical Society in Cedar Run, Iowa. She was looking for help in preparing a special exhibition on her town's contributions to the Civil War.

> *We have in our collection from years ago some documents and other items that belonged to one of our citizens. We know he served in the Civil War, but in checking around we discovered it was not in one of our famed Iowa units. Our examination suggests strongly that it was a Connecticut unit in which he served. The materials say that he was recruited from the town of East Preston, where he presumably then lived. Could you help us out with any information about this man? His name was Albert Randolph.*

His name was Albert Randolph.

They waited until they were outside before doing a quiet but most forceful high five.

"Congratulations, Doctor Spaniel," said Reg.

"Well done, Doctor Womach," said Don. "I hate it that I couldn't resolve the Colt pistol issue, though. . . ."

But off they went in a brisk walk toward their car in the cemetery parking lot.

Reg was the first to spot a man running toward them from the south side of the green. He was at least forty yards away, but it was clear he was waving at them to stop.

"You do the talking," Reg said to Don as they halted and waited. "This is your mission."

"This is history's mission," said Don. Reg laughed. Don did not.

"Welcome to East Preston, Connecticut," said the man as he approached. He extended his right hand, first to Reg and then to Don. "I'm Fred Mackenzie."

Mackenzie. Fred Mackenzie. As in Roland F. Mackenzie?

To Don's eye, the man certainly fit the appearance of a prominent citizen's kin. Fred Mackenzie was a smiling, well-dressed man, about Don's own age. He was wearing a dark blue suit, white shirt, and a bright red tie. His brown hair was full but cut short, his body thin and trim, his demeanor and presence that of substance and confidence.

"We are a small town, and news travels like the wind through it," said Mackenzie, trying, it seemed to Don, to be more casual and light than he really felt. "I hear you two are interested in our Civil War history."

Don confirmed that was absolutely right. "I'm Don Spaniel of the National Park Service in Washington," he said, trying to match Mackenzie for offhanded casualness. "He's Reg Womach. He works for the Smithsonian."

Don imagined he saw questions leaping into Mackenzie's mind. *The National Park Service? The Smithsonian? What is going on here?* And he definitely observed a tinge of color appear in Mackenzie's cheeks.

But before Mackenzie could say anything in response, another man appeared—seemingly out of nowhere—from behind Don and Reg.

"Hi, Jim," said Mackenzie. "These two gentlemen are from Washington—the National Park Service and the Smithsonian. I was just about to ask them about their purpose here."

There was now neither a smile on Mackenzie's face nor in his voice. Don couldn't tell if the abrupt change was brought on by the news about the Park Service and the Smithsonian or by the coming of this other man.

The new arrival was also in a coat and tie—a tweed sport coat and dark slacks. It was an outfit, thought Don, that was slightly out of sync with this warm, sunny July day. But it was New England, after all.

"I'm Jim Allbritten," said the man.

Allbritten. As in Kenneth L. Allbritten?

East Preston was indeed a small town with a wind of news that traveled to all parts, all ears.

Jim Allbritten was huskier, more solid and muscular than Fred Mackenzie. They were both around five foot eleven, but Allbritten outweighed Mackenzie by twenty pounds, and that made him appear shorter. Both were clearly in their late thirties and still had full heads of hair—Fred Mackenzie's a slightly darker brown than Jim Allbritten's—which they wore in similar close cuts.

Don, suddenly on guard, said: "The remains of a Union soldier were found buried on a farm near the battlefield at Antietam in Maryland—"

"Where exactly?" interrupted Mackenzie. "What part of the battlefield?"

"Burnside Bridge."

"My great-great-grandfather was killed at Burnside Bridge," said Jim Allbritten. There was an element of pride in the way he said it. His shoulders came back, his chin went down.

"*My* great-great-grandfather was in that battle, too," said Fred

Mackenzie, matching Allbritten's body language in making the pronouncement.

Neither looked at the other while each spoke.

Don said quickly, "I know. Our research developed the fact that there was a group of ten men in the Eleventh Connecticut who came from East Preston. That's what brought us here today, to try to see if, by chance, the remains might be that of a soldier from here."

"What have you found out?" Mackenzie asked.

"We're still at it. We've reached no conclusions."

"What happens if you do?" It was Allbritten. They were alternating, like two lawyers sharing a witness examination.

"We will make an attempt to find descendants of the identified man and ascertain their wishes about a reburial and a possible ceremony."

"We have a ceremony here on this green every Memorial Day—the names of our great-great-grandfathers are always mentioned," Mackenzie said. "Our town has contributed much blood to our wars."

He paused and said: "I understand you were reading about Roland Mackenzie at the historical society. He lived to a ripe old age here in town. So those remains certainly couldn't be his."

Allbritten said, "Why the great interest in somebody named Albert Randolph?"

He and Mackenzie stopped talking and stared at Don and Reg.

"As I told a man the other day, I come from the vacuum-cleaner school of archeology," Don lied, borrowing Colonel Doleman's approach as his own. He turned ever so gently in the direction of the parking lot. "I believe in scooping up everything in sight."

Allbritten said: "Why did you scoop up a copy of my great-

great-grandfather's photograph? Kenneth L. Allbritten is buried right over there in the cemetery. Your remains surely couldn't be his either."

Don shrugged, determined not to say anything else.

"If you wanted a photo, you could have asked me," Allbritten said. "I have a better one, even, of him in his Civil War uniform—holding his pistol across his chest."

Don took a quick breath and fought off the urge to look at Reg.

"A pistol—what make was it?" he asked Allbritten. "As an archeologist, those kinds of details interest me."

Don hoped he wasn't giving away the spasms that were careening through his insides at the moment.

"It was a Colt," Allbritten said, warming up. He clearly loved talking about his great-great-grandfather. "I read about it in some old letters."

"Colt's a Connecticut company, headquartered in Hartford," Mackenzie said. "I'm sure everybody from here carried Colts."

"Do you happen to know the specific model?" Don asked Allbritten.

"I don't, really. All I remember is that it was a big deal—according to what I read—because Kenneth Allbritten's father, my great-great-*great*-grandfather, gave it to him as a special going-to-war gift. It must have been nonissue and expensive."

Don still didn't even try to steal a glance toward Reg. But he could feel the tension in his usually cool, loose friend.

Don said to Allbritten, "Could it have been a *Police* Colt?"

Allbritten slowly began to nod. "Right, that was it. I recall thinking how interesting that was. . . ."

"Well, good luck, gentlemen, on your mission," Mackenzie said. "Let us know if we can do anything to help—particularly if you end up having a ceremony here."

Allbritten moved his head and eyes in silent agreement.

He and Mackenzie shook hands with Don and Reg and left in different directions—without a wave or a word between them.

It was then, and only then, that Don and Reg faced each other. They exchanged grins and a high five that had twice the spirit and velocity of their earlier one.

"Pardon me while I shout," Don said.

"Let's just quietly get out of here," said Reg.

They continued their walk toward the cemetery.

"I think our bones are Kenneth Allbritten's," said Don.

"Amen," Reg said. "And we owe it all to my brilliant clue about his broken arm."

"And I think those two men know something about how he died," Don said.

"Probably," said Reg. "But I also think there's a lot more bad history going on between them than the battle of Antietam."

When Don didn't immediately ask a follow-up, Reg added: "I think they despise each other."

While he might not have expressed it quite as strongly, Don had also picked up a sense of trouble between Fred Mackenzie and Jim Allbritten. But he said nothing.

Don's racing mind was on Albert Randolph, a photograph—and, mostly, a pistol.

Back again at the high ground, Lieutenant Kenneth L. Allbritten assumed command. He ordered us to take cover in a ravine off to the side of the hill that would provide us some protection from the continuing onslaught of Reb cannon fire. Four of us from East Preston gathered around our lieutenant.

The four of us were Corporal Joseph Campbell, Corporal Roland Mackenzie, Private Charles Jennings, and me, Sergeant Albert Randolph. We were forever mindful that it was through Kenneth Allbritten's words and encouragement that many of us from East Preston chose to answer the call from the Eleventh Connecticut. That common personal history drew the four of us to him as he sought to decide the next course of action for our unit. Our killed and wounded, in the ranks as well as our officer corps, were numerous, wrenching. We all felt terror and foreboding as well as our sense of duty to our divided country and to our state.

It was while we talked to Lieutenant Allbritten that a messenger arrived from headquarters. The messenger, also a lieutenant, was even younger, it seemed, than Kenneth Allbritten. There was a freshness in his face and clean uniform that seemed almost out of place here with us, with the saddened, broken and torn, unkempt and reeling soldiers of the Eleventh Connecticut. He dismounted.

I was struck with disbelief as he told our Lieutenant Allbritten that another assault on the bridge should be launched immediately. He said that was the personal command of General Burnside. He made it sound as if the order had been endorsed and countersigned by the Almighty himself. We, even in our sheltered location, were continuing to be hounded by Rebel musketry and cannon fire from the other side of the creek. The air remained full of hot lead, smoke, and screams. Our nostrils were still packed with the odor of limbs and insides that had been torn from the bodies of friends. I was unbelieving that such an order to go again had come to us.

The messenger turned back toward his horse, and I was preparing to express my disbelief to Lieutenant Allbritten. Before I could speak, a Rebel cannon shot hit the messenger-lieutenant and threw him back toward us. We all rushed to him, and what we saw was a dead man with no head.

The sight of what remained of his neck and shoulders and the scattered grisly remnants of what had been this young man's handsome face was at that moment forever burned into my being. I have never described those sights to another person, and I will not do so now.

I would caution all who wish to remain stable and sane not even to consider opening their imaginations to such views.

Lieutenant Allbritten, in a tone higher than the screech of a panicked cat, ordered us to make ready. The blue of his blue eyes, it seemed, was now almost entirely obscured by those red loops. Every limb of his body was shaking.

"Charge! Toward the bridge! Charge!" He screamed those words at me and the three other fellows from East Preston. His manner was that of a crazed man.

None of the four of us moved. In the stead, each of us argued vehemently against another assault on the bridge. We pleaded for a commonsense understanding that such a course of action would surely result in the wounding or death of us all.

I was shocked at Kenneth Allbritten's adamant, emotional unwillingness to heed our arguments. The redness in his eyes seemed to spread out into his face and down to his neck as if he had been overcome by a torrid fever that had afflicted his entire body.

He pointed at the headless messenger-lieutenant and then to us. "Onward! I hereby order you! The bridge! For his sake! For the sake of Colonel Kingsbury! For the sake of Captain

Griswold! For our *sake*! For the sake of the Union! For God's sake!"

His screams, I reckoned, were so piercingly loud that the Georgians on the bluff pouring lead upon us could have heard them over the sounds of their own weaponry.

Again, none of the four of us, his friends and comrades from his own beloved town, made a motion to assemble.

He let out a cry of distress and loathing, removed his Colt revolver from his holster, waved it high over his head, and took a step from us toward the rest of our unit in the distance, in what, to me and clearly to my three comrades, would be an effort to rally them to the call we had refused to heed.

With no words and only a few glances between the four of us, we made a decision, to wit: Lieutenant Kenneth Allbritten, one of us from East Preston whom we had known since we first set toe and spirit on this earth, had changed from his normal being as a man of intellect, compassion, and bravery. He was now irrational, out of control—yes, insane. Only an insane man would even entertain following the insane order of General Burnside, a man I, along with the rest of the world, would find out later made many foolish command decisions at Antietam, Fredericksburg, and elsewhere that caused the needless death of many a brave and loyal Union soldier. Lieutenant Allbritten was clearly at this moment unable to function as a responsible officer making responsible and logical decisions and issuing responsible and logical orders. Despite the obvious fact that death awaited anyone who would attempt again to take the bridge, he ordered us to do so. He shouted the orders in a manner that indicated beyond a doubt that he was not of his right mind. They were screamed in a voice that was thin and shrieking, like the tightest and highest string on a violin. His arms were waving to and fro as if he had *lost control. It was true that he had seen much death and maiming, and, in fact, we had all witnessed a most horrible death from a cannon shot only moments before.*

But there was no question that, however legitimate the cause of the insanity, it could not be allowed to reign.

8

Don's first act at the office the morning after Connecticut was to ask the Park Service travel people to check the cost of a trip to Iowa. He wanted to go tomorrow or the next day, but there were no discount fares available to Des Moines on such short notice. Furthermore, Cedar Run was an hour and a half by car from Des Moines, and that meant another rental car plus the cost of one night, possibly two, in a motel.

The regional administrator took about two seconds to decline to authorize $1,850 on an emergency basis. Too much money, not enough emergency, said the administrator.

So he telephoned the woman in Cedar Run, Iowa. He had copied down her name and number from the letter she wrote inquiring about Albert Randolph.

"Historical Society, this is Rebecca Fentress," came the voice on the phone after the first ring.

Don identified himself as an archeologist with the National Park Service and got right to the point. "I am looking into the story of a man who lived in your town. He was a veteran of the Civil War. I believe you sent an inquiry about him to the historical society in East Preston, Connecticut."

"Why would the National Park Service be interested in something like that?" she said. "I thought you fine folks concerned yourselves with Yellowstone and the Grand Canyon and Mount Rushmore kinds of attractions." Her tone was cautious, wary. Her voice was definitely that of a mature woman—probably as old as her historical-society counterpart in East Preston.

Don chose his words carefully. "It has to do with a project we have under way involving the found remains of a man who may have died in the battle of Antietam."

Don waited for some response. He got none.

He continued: "I am particularly interested in information about a man named Albert Randolph. I understand that he lived in your town. Is that right?"

"What makes you think he might have?"

"Well, that's what I understand you said in your letter to Connecticut."

"I wrote to them nearly two years ago and never received an answer."

"I'm sorry."

Again, he waited in vain for a volunteered comment or offering.

He plunged on. "The letter—*your* letter—said you had some papers and other material that belonged to Albert Randolph. I would love to examine those—"

"Why?"

"Well, if our information is correct, Albert Randolph fought with the Eleventh Connecticut Volunteer Regiment at Antietam. Those papers might help us shed some light on the identity of the remains we have."

"How do I know you are really with the National Park Service?"

"I could give you a phone number and you could call me back—"

"I've seen all of that on television. That kind of thing is easy to fake. Write me a letter."

"Gladly, yes, ma'am. I will make a formal request for you to send me copies of the material, if that is all right. I am not sure I can come to Iowa anytime soon."

She said firmly: "We do not permit the copying of those papers."

"Why is that, may I ask?"

"They're too sensitive."

Don felt his stomach tightening. "Sensitive? How do you mean that?"

"I mean what *sensitive* means."

Don decided to try one more question. "Would you mind being a little more specific about why they are sensitive?" he asked.

"Yes, I do mind. They're also definitive. I won't explain why they're that either. Write me your letter. After I receive it I will deal with it."

Don had the letter written and on its way within an hour. He paid the $14.50 out of his own pocket for it to go Federal Express overnight.

The FBI also moved quickly on the photo. Don was at the side of Johnny "Cecil B." Howell just after two o'clock on the third afternoon after his return from Connecticut. Howell was the chief video-camera and tape man—known officially as a visual-information specialist—in the FBI lab's photo-imaging division. The high-quality images he could pull out of faded photos, singed documents, and other items was considered miraculous. That, Reg had told Don, was why they called this thirty-two-year-old black man from Birmingham, Alabama, "Cecil B.," as in the great late moviemaker, Cecil B. DeMille.

Again, Reg had taken a pass on coming into the FBI building, but he said it wasn't just his ex-wife problem. He was thinking about joining a war-crimes ID team in Bosnia, and he had to "clear the decks"—meaning his lab tables of unidentified bones—before leaving. Bosnia? Don didn't really buy that. Reg had not mentioned it during their day together on the Connecticut mission. But it didn't matter.

Reg's forensic-anthropologist colleague, Dick Richardson, was present. So was a young research assistant named Joan Williburton. With Don and Howell, they were in a small room that was lit brightly, like a television studio.

Richardson sat at a PC terminal and monitor, and Howell stood to his right behind a video camera. Williburton was ready to assist. Don watched—and hoped.

On Howell's signal, Williburton placed the black-and-white photograph of Kenneth L. Allbritten under brackets on a stationary pedestal in front of the video camera. Working together, Richardson on the computer and Howell on the camera adjusted the picture until it filled two thirds of the computer screen.

Richardson, using software programmed for this kind of thing, hit the right computer keys to digitize the image and store it in the computer. He then taped a large sheet of transparent plastic over the monitor and, using a black grease pencil, traced the major contours of the face, the base of the nose, the borders of the eyes and nose, and other prominent characteristics onto the plastic.

He said, "OK, Johnny, off with the photo."

The photograph of Allbritten disappeared from the computer screen.

"Let's have the real one now," he said to Williburton.

She placed the Burnside skull, the one with two bullet holes, into a doughnut-type ring in front of the camera.

Howell moved the camera into focus as Williburton, following quietly stated commands from Richardson at the computer, moved the skull around. A little to the right and down. No, too much. Back a hair to the left.

Then, finally, Richardson said: "Got it."

Don, watching from behind Richardson, saw the video image of the skull brought to the same size as that in the photograph.

Richardson removed the plastic sheeting and said: "Let's see now what it all looks like."

Again, he went to the computer keyboard and brought the images of both the photograph and the skull to the screen at the same time, superimposing one on the other.

Howell pulled a chair up, and the two of them looked and talked quietly, almost in whispers, while moving the images from one side to the other, from one intensity to another.

Don watched and tried to listen. But he couldn't hear anything he could understand. His breathing became irregular. He felt some rumbling in his stomach.

Ten minutes went by. Another two.

Then Richardson said in full voice to Howell: "What do you think, Cecil B.?"

"They are one and the same, is what I think," Howell said.

"Me, too," Richardson said.

Don heard that loud and clear. His eyes sent a thank-you to the heavens, his breathing went steady and fast.

Richardson turned to him and began explaining all of the detailed superimposed matches in the cranium and the mandible and then specifically the fourteen facial bones, most particularly the superficial ones that make up the upper and lower jaws and the zygomatic bones that form the shape and prominence of the cheeks. . . .

Don did his best to fake interest.

But he had already heard what he came to hear.

They are one and the same, is what I think.

And after several seconds of Richardson's details Don held up his hand to signal for a pause—a stop. He said he was sorry, but could he be excused for a moment?

Without waiting for a response, he ran out of Howell's lab to the first telephone he found.

"They are one and the same!" he shouted to Reg a few seconds later.

It was Corporal Campbell who made the first move. He grabbed Lieutenant Allbritten's right arm and hand and wrested away the Colt pistol that he was waving about. Private Jennings then grabbed the other arm and held it fast against the lieutenant's side. Alarmed at the loudness of the lieutenant's screeching, I stuffed a large cotton bandage into his mouth.

Roland Mackenzie then removed a leather strap from his knapsack and used it to join Lieutenant Allbritten's two hands together behind his back. We then lay him down on the ground, face first.

"We can't just leave him here tied up like this," said Campbell.

"He'll turn us in, and we'll be shot when this is over," Jennings said.

"Yes," I said, "if we untie him he arrests us or he leads us back down that hill and we'll be shot by the Rebs."

There were the most awful noises still coming at us from all di-

rections. There remained people, surely fellow soldiers of the Army of the Potomac, out there on the field of battle yelling and screaming and moaning. The shots from the Confederate cannon banged when they were fired, whistled through the air, and crashed when they landed on something or some person—some one of us. The Confederate rifles popped. Our weapons fired in return.

"This man is crazy!" shouted Mackenzie.

"He'll get us all killed!" yelled Campbell.

"We cannot let him do it!" Jennings said. "We owe it to God to stop him."

I agreed with what they said. I looked at Lieutenant Allbritten's Colt pistol in Campbell's hand. I pointed toward Lieutenant Allbritten and said: "Shoot him. Shoot him with his own gun."

Campbell broke down and cried, poor man. "No, no. I cannot do that. His mother helped deliver me. Mrs. Allbritten was there with the doctor. . . ."

I looked at Jennings.

He shook his head and looked away. "I know it must be done, maybe, but not by me. I will bear witness, but I will not bear the burden."

"What about you, Albert?" Mackenzie then said to me. Impulsively, I reached over and took the Colt revolver from Campbell. I pointed the pistol downward, right in the middle of the back of Lieutenant Allbritten.

"In the head," said Campbell. "Aim higher up."

I moved the barrel of the pistol up to where it was just over Lieutenant Allbritten's head.

The noise of war went on around us, but we did not hear it at that moment. We heard only our own hearts and minds and souls.

"I can't," said I. "I cannot kill this man."

At that moment, I felt another hand on my right hand, the one holding the pistol. It was Roland Mackenzie's. He moved my hand and pistol down to where the barrel was tight up against the base of Kenneth Allbritten's skull. I gave no resistance. Then there was pressure from another finger on my right index finger. There was the cracking explosive sound of the pistol firing. The body of Kenneth Allbritten jerked and twitched once and then again as if touched by a hot ember and then was still.

Then came the Newberne hospital match. Marjorie Reston had been working on it since Don had returned with his notes and possibilities from Carlisle.

She came to Don's office the very morning after the excitement of the FBI photo finding. She first presented him with photocopies of two 1862 Union army medical records from a makeshift Union hospital called the Dixon-Stevenson House in what was then called Newberne, North Carolina.

One showed that T. L. Flintson of the Twenty-third Massachusetts Volunteers, the soldier whose disk was found in the Burnside grave, was a patient there from March 14, 1862, until his death on March 31, 1862.

The other concerned Corporal Joseph Howard Campbell of the Eleventh Connecticut Volunteer Regiment, the East Preston man who had written in his diary about his awful experience in a Newberne hospital. The record said Campbell was under care at the Dixon-Stevenson facility from March 25 to April 5, 1862, when he was declared well from a bullet wound to his left shoulder and deemed fit to return to his unit.

Don scooted his chair over to a table in his office where he had laid out most of the material he and others had collected in the Burnside search.

He found Campbell's name on the handwritten statue list. He was one of the seven boys of East Preston who died in the Civil War. But scanning a photocopied list from a Carlisle book, Don saw that Campbell was not one of those from the Eleventh Connecticut who died with Kingsbury, Griswold, Allbritten, and the others at Burnside Bridge. Then in a note from the Carlisle curator he had read before, Don was reminded that Campbell had survived the worst, the bridge crossing, and then was killed later in the day.

The important finding here, though, was that Corporal Joseph Howard Campbell, for some unknown reason under some unknown circumstance, was in a position to have taken possession of that dead Massachusetts soldier's ID disk while they were both at that house-hospital in Newberne.

All right, let's say Campbell had the disk. Then what? Don asked himself. *How—and why—three months later did it end up with the remains of Lieutenant Kenneth Leonard Allbritten?*

Don felt he was getting close to some final answers.

"Just a little bit longer, Union soldier, and I'll know for certain the details of your killing," he said aloud. "And you know something, from here on I'm going to call you by your real name, Lieutenant Allbritten—Lieutenant Kenneth Leonard Allbritten of East Preston, Connecticut."

Don had forgotten Marjorie Reston. She was still in his office, sitting in a chair next to him at the table. "You didn't hear that," he said to her.

She only smiled.

It flashed into his mind that here was the first woman he had ever met who didn't think it odd that he spoke out loud to a dead Civil War soldier. Could Faye Lee Sutton be the second such woman?

Right now he tried to imagine being married to Marjorie Reston, this bright woman in a two-tone green Park Service uniform. Or just being in bed with her—naked. Or even taking her to the movies or a dinner at a nice restaurant—maybe one of the new places near his apartment in Shirlington Village.

For once, his imagination failed him.

It was the next afternoon that Rebecca Fentress of Cedar Run, Iowa, called from Union Station.

There were no other men of the Eleventh Connecticut close enough to have borne easy witness to our crime. Those in the distance who might have had a vantage point were caught up in their own chaos and confusion of battle and survival.

We four spoke no words and ignored the blood that flowed from the hole in Kenneth Allbritten's head as we quickly moved his body. We carried him out of the ravine, back up to the original high ground whence our first assault had begun. There were trees covering the area, and it was deserted of all other soldiers.

Digging feverishly and in tandem with our hands and weapons, we created a deep grave. I cannot accurately recount the time taken to complete the task, but it seemed to be over much more quickly than common thought would have forecast. The horror of what we had done and the fear of being found out no doubt spurred us to dig at a speed well beyond what would be considered usual. The feverishness of our labor is all that I remember. I cannot bring to my mind's eye the sight or feel of one handful of dirt that I removed in order to make a place for Kenneth Allbritten.

I do know for a certainty that while digging we left him face-down on the ground so as not to have to gaze at his face, a feat I knew I would be unable to accomplish. He remained that way as we removed his ID disk from his neck by pulling it off with its chain from behind and emptied his pockets of two letters we could see were from members of his beloved family in East Preston.

Still keeping his eyes downward, his limbs bound and mouth gagged, we lowered his body into the grave. Corporal Joseph Campbell held up an ID disk for us all to see and then dropped it down onto Lieutenant Allbritten's remains. Corporal Campbell said he had picked up the disk when he was treated at a field hospital after our involvement in the battle for Newberne, North Carolina. He said it belonged to a man from the Twenty-third Massachusetts and that he found it after the man had died from his wound and the corpse of the man had been removed from a location on the floor near his own. He said he'd intended to return it to the dead Massachusetts man's family when this awful war was done.

Then, with the same swiftness that had marked our digging of the grave, we covered up the remains of our fallen comrade, our victim.

I am ashamed of so much of what we did during those few minutes, but I am most ashamed of the fact that none of us thought to say a word of prayer, of benediction, of remorse, of delivery. We made no request of God in Heaven to bless the soul *of Kenneth Allbritten, to bless the life he had lived on earth, to now take this faithful son into the Kingdom of Heaven in the name of our savior, the Lord Jesus Christ. We were already murderers, and now our rush to avoid discovery had transformed us into an even more loathsome form of subhuman godless creatures.*

We returned to the scene of our crime. Our task was to ensure that all but a most unlikely close inspection of the messenger-lieutenant's headless remains would show those remains to be those of Lieutenant Allbritten. We removed the messenger's own ID disk and stuck Lieutenant Allbritten's ID disk down the front of the other man's dark blue tunic. We placed Lieutenant Allbritten's letters in one of the trouser pockets. The blood and gore of the death made these gaggingly unpleasant tasks, but the awfulness also covered much of the dead man's uniform and obscured his buttons, making it most unlikely, if not impossible, for an interested party to ascertain a difference between the uniform of a lieutenant from the Eleventh Connecticut and that of the messenger-lieutenant's unit, the identity of which we were unaware.

We told our immediate world of the Eleventh Connecticut and the larger world of the Union army then—and later the one of our beloved East Preston—the story of the messenger-lieutenant's terrible death as if it had happened to Lieutenant Allbritten. When asked by military officers at the end of that day of September 17 if we had ever seen a certain messenger-lieutenant, we replied in the negative. I assume he was considered a victim and a missing person from that chaos and confusion and tragedy of the battle. Jennings rid us of this unfortunate man's ID disk by later throwing it into that creek called the Antietam, a name that I knew on that day would live on in history. I have no idea now who that young officer was. I grieve for his family.

I grieve for the family of Kenneth Allbritten. I grieve for my soul and those of my three conspirators. Two of them, Campbell and Jennings, were struck down later that September 17 in the last engagements with Rebel forces before dark came to quiet the cannons and the rifles and to stop the killing and the maiming. Jennings was killed instantly with a musket shot through his head in the last confrontation with the Confederates near the Harper's Ferry Road. Campbell suffered a chest wound an hour earlier from a cannon shot and died at a field hospital in a Sharpsburg church four days later.

Roland Mackenzie and I returned to East Preston when the war ended, and we were discharged from service in the Eleventh Connecticut. We never spoke of the Lieutenant Allbritten incident, and the good citizens of our community made heroes of us and, more so, of Lieutenant Allbritten, who gave his life on the field of battle at Antietam. I would regularly cross paths of society and commerce with Roland, and our eyes would meet and lock, and then he would smile, and I would nod, and we would go about our chores. After what seemed as if it were ten thousand times meeting thus, I began to seek ways to avoid such encounters of the eyes and soul. I left East Preston a few years afterward because I could no longer bear the burden of the crime we had committed and the lies I was living in its wake. I could no longer withstand the paralyzing shocks of painful guilt that permeated me whenever my gaze fell upon Kenneth's widow or now fatherless child. I saw them much less often than I did Roland, but it was horrendously jarring to my being when I did so.

I had hoped and prayed that coming here to Iowa, to a new life away from the constant reminders of my deeds and sins, would lead to a peace that would make it possible for me to live a life worth living. That has not been the case. There has been no rest. I have spent hours in private torment grappling with the exalted *idea that Kenneth Allbritten had to die in order to save the lives of others. I do not make that plea of justification now because it has no weight, no worth, and, as a consequence, neither do I have weight or worth.*

I would finish this with words of prayer, with a plea to my God for understanding and forgiveness if I thought I merited same. I do not.

Albert Randolph

PART TWO

TAPS

9

"Albert Randolph."

Don sat still and quiet amid the crowds and noise at Union Station. He read the signature once, twice. Mumbled it, mouthed it. Touched it with his hand.

Now he knew what had happened. Exactly how it was done and why. A wave of pleasure careened through him. Congratulations, Doctor Spaniel, on a job well done. Mission accomplished.

And from his Union Station waiting-room seat he looked in the direction of Iowa. *This, Ms. Fentress, is one of those exquisite professional moments that fulfills me in what I do. Thank you, thank you, thank you, for making it possible.*

He raced his eyes back through what Randolph had called his "terrible words of confession."

"I was party to one of the most heinous crimes the darkest side of the human spirit can generate." Those words were right at the beginning.

My God, yes. My God. What a story, what a drama—but, yes, what a travesty, what a crime! They murdered that kid lieutenant in cold blood. They executed him. He was their friend from childhood. How appalling, how horrible—how intolerable. How dare they.

He was anxious to call Reg, to share his rage and pleasure, to talk about what to do about it.

But first there were the other items in Ms. Fentress's envelope.

There was a typewritten statement and list that was dated March 24, 1961—just over thirty years ago.

> To whom it may concern,
>
> The following items were found in a sealed cast-iron container that was buried in a flower bed on the Randolph Homestead property in Cedar Run, Iowa. There were no known owners or resulting claimants, so the contents were given to the Marion County Historical Society and Museum.
>
> The items:
>
> —Union army ID disk, name, Albert Randolph, Eleventh Connecticut Volunteer Regiment
>
> —Union army sergeant's insignia, with boots and belt
>
> —Official honorable discharge of Sergeant Albert Randolph from the Army of the United States
>
> —Sealed envelope containing unknown papers
>
> —Black-and-white photo of Albert Randolph
>
> T. Whitfield Davidson
Sheriff, Marion County, Iowa

The discharge was an Eagle discharge paper, so called because there was the symbol of a winged eagle with three flags at the top below the words: "To all whom it may concern." It was a certificate-like paper that had blanks to fill in for the individual soldier.

Know ye, that Albert Randolph, Sergeant, of the Eleventh Connecticut Volunteers, was discharged from service to the United States on the 22d day of November in the year 1865. He had been enrolled into the army at Hartford four years and one month before.

Said Albert Randolph was born in East Preston in the state of Connecticut, is 22 years of age, five feet nine inches high, fair complexion, gray eyes, brown hair, and by occupation, when enrolled, a student.

On the back of the suitable-for-framing document was a justice-of-the-peace certification and stamp, which officially stated that the man who received this document and his final pay was indeed Albert Randolph.

Next, there was a reproduction of a small newspaper clipping that had been pasted into the center of a piece of regular white copy paper. It was an obituary of Albert Randolph.

LOCAL MERCHANT

PASSES AWAY

UNEXPECTEDLY

Then came the story.

Albert Randolph died in this city yesterday. He was a well-known person in Cedar Run as the owner of Randolph's, the jewelry, furniture, and housewares store on the square.

He came to our city six years ago from Connecticut. He was a faithful Christian and a member of the Methodist Church and the Masons. He was a veteran of the Civil War, having served in the Union army during various important battles as a member of a volunteer regiment from Connecticut.

He had no family that were known in Cedar Run.

Funeral services will be on Wednesday with burial to follow in the cemetery at the church.

The last item in Ms. Fentress's envelope was the photograph of Albert Randolph. It was a head shot of a man in his twenties, dressed in a wing-collared white shirt and dark dress coat. He was looking off solemnly to his left with eyes that, from the discharge paper, Don knew to be gray. His hair was wavy, perfectly combed. So was the heavy mustache that hung down on both sides from above his closed lips.

There was no date on the picture, but, because he was not in uniform, it most probably was taken after the war.

Don stared hard at this man. What can you tell about a person's soul from a photograph? *What kind of man were you really, Albert Randolph? Were you a troubled spirit even before Antietam, before Burnside Bridge—before you helped fire a round into Kenneth Allbritten's skull?*

And Don immediately thought of Jack Hyland, a forensic pathologist in Iowa with whom he had done some business in the past. Jack might be able to find out, just for the record to complete the story, Albert Randolph's own cause of death.

Don got Hyland's Des Moines listing from his address book and dialed the number on his cell phone.

Hyland was there. And he said most of that kind of cause-of-death information was now on a slick new computer system, but he was not sure how far back the entries went.

Don listened to the click of a computer keyboard for a few seconds. Then Hyland said, "Here he is. Albert Randolph died on September 17, 1872, in Cedar Run, Marion County. I found him in a special computer category because of the cause of death."

"What was that?" Don asked.

"Suicide. Some graduate students at Iowa State several years ago did a study of suicide on the farm. They compiled all of the suicides going back to the beginning of Iowa."

"And in Randolph's case?"

"Well, there was an investigation by the local sheriff, apparently."

"How did the guy kill himself?"

"Let me see. . . ."

Don listened again to the sound of computer keys being struck.

Hyland said: "Well, Don, all it says is gunshot." There was a pause and more computer clicks. "No, here it is. He stuck a shotgun in his mouth and blew his head off. Is that what you wanted to know?"

"Yes, Jack. Yes. Thanks . . ."

"You OK?"

"I'm fine. Thanks. I owe you one."

"You sound funny—suddenly."

Don resisted saying: "I *feel* funny—suddenly."

But Hyland now wanted to chat about other things. They had last talked two years ago when Don was asked by Hyland's office to help identify some Civil War artifacts—handguns, bayonets, buttons, and buckles—that had turned up during some interstate-highway construction in western Iowa.

Don did not want to chat. He wanted to call Reg. He wanted to think.

Albert Randolph. He and his three Connecticut buddies summarily execute their commanding officer, a man they have known all their lives. They do so because they believe he has gone crazy and would lead them and their unit to certain death.

Ten years later to the day, tormented and unable to cope with his guilt and goblins, Albert Randolph writes out a personal confession, places it in an airtight metal box with some of his Civil War mementos, and buries it. Then he blows his brains out.

For Don, everything had suddenly changed. The aching issues no longer concerned solving mysteries or practicing archeology.

They were only what he did now with and about the story of Albert Randolph, Kenneth Allbritten, and their comrades of the Eleventh Connecticut. He recalled—with clarity—Rebecca Fentress's question about his being prepared to deal with the consequences of knowing Randolph's story.

And now he will call Reg.

No, that can wait until he is back at the office. Take some deep breaths, cool down, absorb what happened.

Reg will be great in helping figure out how to proceed and how to remain calm and professional while doing so. So will Colonel Doleman.

But as he walked to his car in the Union Station parking garage, Don's thoughts returned again and again to those two men on the East Preston green: Jim Allbritten and Fred Mackenzie.

Don chose a small island in the middle of the Potomac River for his what-next meeting with Reg. It was Theodore Roosevelt Island, dedicated to the great man's name and achievements. Don knew Reg's early interest and devotion to TR had never waned. He continued to talk about him and to read everything that was written about him, including most particularly the biographies by David McCullough, Edmund Morris, and Nathan Miller.

There was also a Civil War angle to the island, which was between the John F. Kennedy Center for the Performing Arts on the D.C. side of the Potomac and Rosslyn in Virginia. A volunteer regiment of black troops marched and trained on this island—it was then called Mason's Island—after the battle of Antietam and after the Emancipation Proclamation was issued. One of Don's archeological predecessors at the Park Service had done some minor digging a few years ago and had turned up a few bullets, ID disks, and other traces of the black soldiers.

And if nothing else, there were more than two miles of nature trails on Theodore Roosevelt Island. The walk would be good for their souls as well as their bodies.

They met at eleven o'clock in the morning in the island's near-empty parking lot. There were seldom many vehicles there because it had only enough spaces for a handful of cars—none for those caravans of school and chartered buses full of tourists and students that are so common in Washington.

"God, I love this place," said Reg, leading the way across a fifty-foot wooden pedestrian bridge, the only access to the island. "Although what I have to say about your professional dilemma, Doctor Spaniel, I could have said in two quick minutes over the phone yesterday right after you told me about Randolph's confession and all the rest. That would have saved both of us much valuable time. I'm trying to get off to Bosnia, you know, next week."

"You're going to be gone a month?"

"At least."

Don said he was grateful for his time and help. He wanted more than just Reg's opinion, though. He needed an airing, some discussion. Reg came at these things differently than he did.

"Leave it alone, that's what I would have said—and what I say now," said Reg, walking them first to the main monument area, where they admired the seventeen-foot-high bronze Paul Manship statue of Teddy Roosevelt. "As the great man himself might have said: Die and let die, live and let live, Don."

"You know better than anybody that Roosevelt would never have said anything like that. He would have said, 'Go!', 'Charge!'—or something similar."

Reg acknowledged the truth of that with a smile.

On the statue, Theodore Roosevelt's left hand was palm up just below his waist; his right hand was palm out above his head.

"What is he supposed to be doing?" Don asked, ignoring—for now—Womach's statement of advice. "He looks like he's playing defense in a basketball game."

"He's making a vigorous speech," Reg said. "He made a speech in my hometown once—"

"While taking a bribe with his left hand?"

"Shame on you, Doctor Spaniel," Reg said with serious and real indignation. "There was never anything like that about Theodore Roosevelt."

And he told Don that speech in Dickinson, North Dakota, which then had a population of only seven hundred or so, was on July 4, 1886. The invitation grew out of a great Roosevelt escapade three months before that quickly became—and remained—part of the permanent TR legend. He had showed up in Dickinson one April morning holding three men at gunpoint that he said had stolen a boat of his. He had chased them for weeks down the Little Missouri River and then brought them by wagon—Roosevelt walking behind the wagon with a Winchester—forty-five miles to Dickinson to turn them in to the sheriff. Why hadn't he just shot them? somebody asked. It never occurred to me, TR replied.

Don loved the story and immediately sought to make it and TR relevant to the business at hand. "There was a vicious and, in my opinion, unjustified battlefield murder at Antietam that went un-noted, and, worse, the result is—as we speak—men resting in other men's graves. Roosevelt would have wanted there to be justice, for the wrongs to be corrected."

Reg said nothing. He led Don behind the statue to four granite tablets that rose out of the ground more than twenty feet into the sky. Each had TR's thoughts about a particular issue or subject.

"TR would have put it right back on you," Reg said. "Why

disturb a peace that has been in place for one hundred and thirty-four years? Who gave you the right to come along and tear that peace all apart? What about those two guys we met up in Connecticut and the other descendants of these dead men? Don't they have the right to be left alone? Don't they have the right to have their family legacies left alone?"

"And I would answer that no one—including Jim Allbritten and Fred Mackenzie—can be immune from the truths of history."

"Not bad, not bad—for a simple man of archeology," said Reg, pointing to some engraved words of Theodore Roosevelt, not a simple man of anything, on "The State" tablet. And he pointedly read them out loud to Don: " 'In popular government results worth having can be achieved only by men who combine worldly ideals with practical good sense.' "

"This is different," Don said.

"Practical good sense is what you need right now, Don. Why not simply declare the remains in my lab as officially 'unknown,' arrange for a small burial ceremony at the national cemetery at Antietam, and walk away from it all? Let the lawyers figure out what happens to the pistol and the rest of the stuff you have. You will have your private satisfactions in knowing that you cracked the case. And you move on, leaving things mostly as you found them."

They started down the hiking path that wound through the trees around the perimeter of the island. It was a couple of yards wide, mostly gravel, pine needles, and fallen leaves that traveled a route shaded by tall dogwood, sycamore, and other trees and outlined by rocks of all sizes on both sides.

Reg kept talking. "Is it right and proper for you, an employee of the National Park Service, to disrupt a settled situation of history? Is it the role of the Smithsonian to have one of its employees—me—help you trigger a potential uproar over something that happened one hundred and thirty-four years ago? Do our respective bosses and supervisors want or need the kind of grief this might bring them? My people, I know for a fact, are particularly raw and sensitive right now because of the *Enola Gay* flap. We work in Washington, but we are not *of* Washington—"

"What does that mean?"

"It means we don't make uproars. They're not our thing."

"We'd clear it with everybody at the Park Service—I'd have to. I can't do a thing on my own."

"What if they denied you permission to proceed?"

Don thought of Rebecca Fentress in Iowa, secretly making a copy of the Randolph papers and slipping off to Washington on the train. "I don't know what I'd do," he said softly.

Off to the left was the Kennedy Center, through the trees. And facing it was a bench, one of several placed at intervals along this path. Without a word, they sat down next to each other.

Reg said, "I have another reason for you to drop it. After you told me yesterday about the Iowa documents and the suicide by Randolph, I asked myself: How did that man, our guy Allbritten, die? From a pistol shot traveling from the occipital bone up through his brain and out the frontal bone of his cranium. What about those remains that are presumably under Allbritten's tombstone in East Preston, Connecticut? The lieutenant-messenger? He died from a cannon shot that obliterated his head. And now there's Albert Randolph, one of the four killers of Allbritten. How did he die? By firing a shotgun into his mouth and up into his skull. That's quite a few people to die pretty much the same way."

"What are you saying, for God's sake?"

"That it's possible for a reasonably normal, cautious person to say: Let's get out of this thing now before something happens to somebody else's cranium."

"You're being ridiculous."

"Maybe not. Maybe there's something going on here that we ordinary scientist-mortals do not understand. Maybe these lethal shots through so many heads have been some power's way of saying, Cool it, Doctor Spaniel. Maybe you should truly let dead soldiers lie. Maybe the power behind it is none other than those remains on my lab table. Maybe these shattered heads are their— his—way of saying, Leave me and everyone else alone, fellas."

Don was on his feet. Suddenly he was moving again. And so was Reg.

"Got to you, didn't I, Don?"

Don said, truthfully, "A little bit, maybe."

"It had already occurred to you on your own, hadn't it?"

Don didn't respond.

"I'll bet you remember what I told you about Jim Allbritten and Fred Mackenzie despising each other."

Don reached down and picked up a rock about the size of a baseball that was off to the side of the path. And he threw the rock in the direction of the Kennedy Center, some four hundred yards away. He did so with such ferocity that he thought for a second it might really go that far, sail high and away over the trees and the river, and land on the roof of the Kennedy Center, named, too, for a man who had had his head split open by a for- eign object. But instead the rock crashed harmlessly into some trees down by the water.

He said, "I don't see how we can take it upon ourselves to de- cide information cannot be disseminated because it might agitate those two men in East Preston or cause someone there to change a story or the name of a school, to edit a tombstone or a street sign. Those decisions are for others to make. We do not make policy, we make facts."

"Facts. Who knows what's a fact?"

"I know what is fact. So do you. We know what happened in that Maryland ravine on September 17, 1862. We owe it to ourselves and everything we stand for as scientists, as fact finders, to disclose those facts."

"I hear ya, 'Harrison.'"

Don glared at Reg. "What are you saying?"

"That you really want to be a star—go on *Larry King* or something."

"This is not about me!"

"Yeah, it is. Let's start walking again."

They moved on for a few minutes. Neither said anything.

"Well?" Womach finally said.

"Well, what?"

"Are you going for the glory?"

Don, his emotional temperature rising, said, "The lieutenant-messenger is a reason enough to proceed. Who was this guy? Who was this guy who had his head blown off and his identity and very being stolen? Doesn't he deserve to have his remains and his legacy resurrected and consecrated?"

"Amen, Harrison," Reg said, clapping his hands together. And then, in an amazingly accurate impersonation of Larry King's lean into the camera, Reg said out across the Potomac: "And now for your calls. If you have anything to ask this brilliant young archeologist, please give us a call at 1-800-BIG-EGOS."

There was red in Don's face, heat throughout his shaking body.

"I'm just a lieutenant-messenger, Don," said Reg. "All I'm doing is passing on what you may need to hear about yourself. You've gotten too close, too involved, too carried away with this. . . ."

Don picked up a rock with both hands and raised it above his head. This rock was large—about the size of a small cushion—jagged edged and sharp pointed.

Reg reflexively raised his left arm to deflect the blow.

Don blinked twice, lowered the rock. "Good God Almighty, Reg. I almost cracked your head open."

"I know, I know."

Both were shaking. Two different men might have embraced.

They walked quickly and silently back over the walkway to the parking lot and drove away in their respective cars.

Don had the instant belief that this would be the last time he would see Colonel Doleman alive. The old man was in bed, in tan silk pajamas and a blue terry-cloth robe, and propped up by pillows. His hair had grown long from not having been cut for a while, his skin was as gray as his hair, and his big brown eyes were watery.

"I am dying a good death, Doctor Spaniel, if that's what the startled look on your otherwise bright face is asking," said the colonel, his voice only a pittance of its once loud and forceful self. "Slipping silently away while being waited on by maidens and minions certainly trumps being torn asunder on a battlefield by a cannonball."

Only the volume was gone, thought Don. The man's power of thought and communication remained intact—as it clearly would till he took his last breath.

Don had been to this house on a side street in Sharpsburg once before. It was one of many structures in town, like Milliken's store, that had some September 17, 1862, history to it. In the original wood, partially covered with white Masonite siding until the colonel bought it ten years ago, were several hundred bullet holes. The story was that Confederate troops used it as headquarters on the nights of the fifteenth and sixteenth before deserting it under heavy Union fire at the end of the seventeenth.

Colonel Doleman and his wife, Rosemary—the primary maiden and minion in his life—had furnished it in the period of the 1860s, from the few rag rugs on the floor to the dark brown Victorian chairs, couches, and lamps. The walls were crowded with sketches and paintings of scenes and soldiers, the open shelves stuffed with books and monographs, the small tables and cupboards cluttered with shells and other fragments—all from the battle that was fought in and near this house more than 130 years ago.

Don had come this morning with some light information along with his serious questions. He had looked up the roots of the phrase *under the weather* in the *Oxford English Dictionary* and was prepared to entertain the colonel with tales of seasickness from ancient literature, in which the expression first began to appear.

But, upon seeing the colonel, Don skipped all of that and got right down to purposes. In forceful, direct language, he sketched out the story of what a few men of the Eleventh Connecticut had done to their hometown friend and last standing leader, Lieutenant Kenneth Allbritten.

The colonel closed his eyes halfway through Don's recitation. And when he finished, for a second, Don had the horrible thought that the great man of Antietam had just drawn his last breath. The story had killed him!

But no. "There is a trace of wrath in your voice, Doctor Spaniel. Have you taken a moral position on what happened?"

"There was no reason to kill the man, colonel—that's the way I see it, at least."

The colonel had yet to open his eyes. But he said, "Passion in the pursuit of truth is just fine. Passion in judging the acts of others in time of uncommon, unimaginable stress may not be so fine."

Don chose not to argue the pros and cons of appropriate passion with this dying man.

And the colonel said, "Whatever your passions, you have truly done unto history what must always be done, Doctor Spaniel." The words were spoken in a slow whisper. Don leaned over and closer to make sure he heard everything right. "You have unearthed a new story, a story that shatters my view of things. I believed that those men on that field of battle—I consider it *my* field of battle—were of a different breed than the rest of mankind. I believed that they acted and behaved with a nobility that was in a magnificent and heroic category of its own. I was wrong, Doctor Spaniel. Of course, I was wrong. I was a fool to have thought otherwise. They were only ordinary men because only ordinary men fight our wars. Oh, what a fool I was. Thank you, Doctor Spaniel. Now please, leave me to my thoughts."

Don could not do so until he had asked the questions he had come to ask. He moved closer to the colonel's ear.

"What do I do about the two sets of remains, colonel?" he said. "Leave them be, or—"

"No!" As if rising from the dead, the colonel raised his head, opened his eyes. The voice was louder, back to at least half of normal. "Put it right! You must put it right! For the sake of the two lieutenants, you must put them in their own graves!"

Don had an important follow-up question. "What about telling the story of what happened in the ravine—do I ask the Park Service to let me make it public? What do I do about that?"

The colonel's head was back on the pillow now, his eyes were again closed. And in the earlier feeble voice, to which he returned, he whispered, "That's up to you, Doctor Spaniel, to do what you feel your duty and purpose require. But if you tell the world, be prepared to deal with the unexpected. The passions and the brutalities of the battlefield, if reawakened, might trigger reactions and aftermaths beyond your control. That is all I have to say. Now, please, leave me be."

Don thanked the colonel and began to turn away.

"One more thing, though, Doctor Spaniel." The colonel was still speaking softly, but Don had no trouble hearing or understanding. "I want my ashes spread at that spot on the bank of the Antietam where Captain Griswold lay down to die."

"Of course, colonel."

"They tell me it's against some kind of federal Park Service rule to do so. . . ."

"I'll see that it's done, colonel. I give you my word in the name of Captain Griswold and the two lieutenants and all of the others who went before you."

The smile on the colonel's face allowed Don to complete his turn and, finally, to leave him be.

Don was confident about his findings but nervous about the show-and-tell meeting, officially scheduled as an "assessment review and action briefing." The director, as well as several other top Park Service people, was going to listen to a presentation from him and then decide the course of his action on the Burnside Remains Matter. That's what it was now being called within the department.

And, if that wasn't enough, Faye Lee Sutton was going to be there. Early on, he had relished the opportunity to work with her again, but his few premeeting phone conversations with her had been most brief and cool. There was no sign she even remotely shared his desire to rekindle their personal relationship.

Now she barely glanced at him as she came into the room—the conference room in the executive offices of the National Park Service. But, to Don's aroused eyes and soul, Faye Lee had never looked better. She was wearing a dark blue two-piece suit kind of thing that fit her perfectly. Her dark brown hair and eyes were superbly matched in color and sparkle.

She took a seat across from him and to his right at the oval table that dominated the room, a place of dark oak walls that, with the table and twelve leather-backed chairs, was equipped today with a slide projector and a large white screen.

Faye Lee began chatting with one and then another of the other five people in the room. Don had already properly greeted them upon his arrival. They included the assistant director for public affairs and the chief archeologist-adviser to the director, as well as Mark Potter, the regional administrator, who had, with good humor, forgiven Don for the Friday-at-Carlisle episode.

In a few seconds, Don gave up trying to make eye contact with Faye Lee, looked down at his notes, and resumed his anxiety over what he was really there to do this afternoon.

And in a few minutes, everyone stood when Jason Krause, the director of the National Park Service, entered. They did so because he was the boss, but Don also knew there was more to it than that. A poet and photographer who specialized in environmental history, he was the first person ever to win the Pulitzer Prize in two different book categories—first, for some poetry on the vanishing rice fields of southern Texas, and again for a collection of essays and photos about the environmental side of the Lewis and Clark expedition up the Missouri River.

Krause was tanned, athletic, and seemed younger than the fifty-five Don knew him to be. Don had never met Krause before this moment because, until now, there had been no reason for their paths to cross. It was not unusual for someone to do Don's kind of work for thirty years and never lay an eye on any director, who was always a political appointee. Don, watching Krause go around the table shaking hands, immediately liked what he saw. He seemed to be an open, warm, gregarious man who, when he got to Don, also appeared genuinely interested in what this meeting was all about.

And a few seconds later, it was show time. Don hit some buttons on the table in front of him. The lights in the room dimmed and color photos of the remains of Kenneth L. Allbritten appeared giant-sized, one after another, on the screen against a far wall. Don had had an NPS graphics-department photographer take two basic overhead shots—with the bones laid out facedown, the way they were found, and faceup. There were also several close-ups of the skull, the wrists, and the right forearm.

"We are here because of these bones that were found by two Civil War relic hunters," Don said. "The bones had a story to tell, and we heard it."

The screen picture changed to the 1861 photo of Kenneth L. Allbritten in his Union officer's uniform.

But before Don could say anything else, Krause said: "I understand this kind of relic hunting has become something quite large."

"That's right," Don said. "There are thousands of people doing it either as a hobby or as a business, and there are swap meets and clubs and newsletters and slick magazines and price guides for one and all."

"What's the attraction?"

"I think for most it's simply an intense interest in our nation's only civil war, one in which many of us had ancestors involved."

"There are some real scum out there in the business," said J. Hancock Larson, the chief NPS archeologist-adviser.

"There are scum in all businesses," Don shot back.

Watch it, Doctor Spaniel, Don said to himself. *This is not about relic hunting. This is about those bones on Reg Womach's lab table, and those remains under that tombstone in East Preston, Connecticut.*

"What about the crazies who do the reenacting?" Larson persisted. "What are grown men doing out there on weekends in blue and gray uniforms and imagining they are real soldiers fighting in a real war more than one hundred and thirty years ago?"

Don and Larson had had this debate before at meetings. Don wasn't about to waste valuable time having it again now. So he only shrugged his shoulders.

But Larson would not leave it alone. "I assume you've read the media reports about some of the Confederate reenactors being racists who believe they are fighting for the cause of white supremacy—and other idiocies."

Don nodded. He had seen the stories.

"Did you read that piece in the *Post* about some reenactors seriously believing they are Civil War soldiers reincarnated?"

Krause, justifying Don's instant admiration for him, interrupted. "Maybe we should allow Doctor Spaniel to proceed with his report?"

Don, guiding everyone's gaze back to the large photo of Allbritten, said: "We concluded from our investigation that those remains were of this man, a twenty-one-year-old lieutenant in the Eleventh Connecticut Volunteer Regiment who died on September 17, 1862, during the battle of Antietam."

He had been told he had no more than fifteen minutes to make the presentation, his case. He hoped the time Larson took just didn't count. But, just in case, he moved quickly through the evidence he had assembled that established the identity of those remains.

The finale was a dramatic one-two shot on the big screen.

The superimposed skull on the photograph of Kenneth L. Allbritten.

Then, a blowup of these sentences from Albert Randolph's handwritten confession:

> *"In the head," said Campbell. "Aim higher up."*
>
> *I moved the barrel of the pistol up to where it was just over Lieutenant Allbritten's head.*
>
> *The noise of war went on around us, but we did not hear it at that moment. We heard only our own hearts and minds and souls.*
>
> *"I can't," said I. "I cannot kill this man."*
>
> *At that moment, I felt another hand on my right hand, the one holding the pistol. It was Roland Mackenzie's. He moved my hand and pistol down to where the barrel was tight up against the base of Kenneth Allbritten's skull. I gave no resistance. Then there was pressure from another finger on my right index finger. There was the cracking explosive sound of the pistol firing. The body of Kenneth Allbritten jerked and twitched once and then again as if touched by a hot ember and then was still.*

Don, for dramatic effect, waited a full count of five before switching the lights back on.

"That is some story, Doctor Spaniel, some story indeed," said Krause.

There was a general rumbling of agreement from the others. Don saw that Faye Lee seemed touched by the story. He thought he even saw a glint of a tear in one of those beautiful eyes.

Krause began clapping, leading the others in a round of applause for Don. That made Don feel terrific, particularly when he noticed that Faye Lee was joining in. And smiling. Don then thanked everyone and started reciting the names of Reg, Marjorie Reston, and others who worked on the project.

Krause moved it on with the question: "Have you identified the lieutenant-messenger, the man whose remains you believe were substituted for the other one?'

"We are still working on that, sir," Don said.

He decided it would be premature to tell them that Marjorie Reston and others had, just in the last two days, come up with a matched man and situation. There was a Lieutenant Richard Allen Rhodes of an Illinois cavalry unit who had been assigned that September 17 to McClellan's headquarters staff. He turned up missing when the day was done and was memorialized as missing in his Illinois hometown when the war was over. Obviously, the real proof would not come until they were able to look at the remains in the Connecticut cemetery. And with Reg now in Bosnia, somebody else at the Smithsonian would have to do that bones work.

Krause then turned to Faye Lee. "It certainly appears Doctor Spaniel has the goods on the first, and most important, part of the mystery. What do we do about it?"

Don now could look at Faye Lee openly—along with everyone else in the room. His interest was most definitely rekindled. He imagined what it might be like to be with her in one of those cozy railway compartments Ms. Fentress had mentioned.

"It is very sensitive from this point on," Faye Lee said. Her voice was feminine but authoritative, soft but firm. Don loved listening to her. "We are prepared to work with the Department of Defense and others to mount a full reburial service with all of the trimmings. But our limited goal is to find an appropriate and discreet way to simply replace the remains now in the Connecticut grave with the real remains of Allbritten. The other remains would be held until Doctor Spaniel and his associates make a definite identification. The most important first step is exhuming the Connecticut cemetery remains. We will work with the appropriate state historical-commission authorities as well as the state attorney general's office in getting that done. We will enlist their assistance and support in procuring the proper permissions and permits to exhume the remains in East Preston."

"I say be very careful as you go about this," said Mike Quinn, the public-affairs man.

Krause said: "Why careful, Mike? How could anyone object to sorting out the proper burial grounds of two men who gave their lives in the Civil War, for God's sake?"

Don knew from his premeeting briefing that Quinn was a prominent political consultant to Democratic candidates. He, like Krause, was known as an old friend of the vice president of the United States.

"Someone is out there, ready to object to everything, Mr. Director," Quinn said. Then he asked Don, "Have you located any descendants of any of these people? That's where the problems could come."

"Allbritten has some direct descendants in East Preston—one in particular who is a prominent attorney. I met him in the course of the investigation a few weeks ago, but I have not told him of our findings."

Quinn said: "Well, all it takes is for him or some other obscure second cousin ten times removed to raise hell with the federal government for wanting to disrupt the peace of their ancestor. What are you going to do about the battlefield murder story?"

"It's quite a story, as the director said, and I, for one, would like to release it to the public," Don said, sensing that the discussion was moving into difficult territory. "That, of course, is the director's decision."

Larson, the anti-reenactor archeologist, said, "That's exactly right, and that's why we're having this meeting." Don and Larson had never gotten along, but it wasn't personal—or even that professional. It was based solely on the bureaucratic fact that Don, to his delight, was answerable to a regional Park Service administrator, who saw Don as the only expert on archeology. Larson thought, to his continual frustration, that all archeology and archeologists in the service should function under him.

Quinn was shaking his head. "Not without the complete and in-writing approval of any and all descendants involved can there be any such storytelling. They might not want the world to know that their ancestors wasted their commanding officer—and friend."

Don put his tongue on full restraint. He did not yell back at Quinn: "This is not for those ancestors to decide. History is history; what happened, happened. Why should two great-great-grandsons, Jim Allbritten and Fred Mackenzie—particularly Mackenzie—have the right to decide this?"

Krause asked Faye Lee for her opinion. "I think Mr. Quinn makes a valid point. There could even be legal ramifications concerning reputations and the like."

Without being asked, of course, Larson agreed. So did the other Park Service officials in the room, who had remained completely silent during the entire meeting.

Krause stood up. All others in the room then rose.

The director came around the table to Don. "Let's do it Mike's way, Doctor Spaniel: carefully, with all permissions, one step at a time."

"You're the boss," Don said, and immediately felt like a fool for doing so.

But, like it or not, the discussion had ended.

"The American people are well served by you," Krause said, still with Don. He looked at Mike Quinn, a sixtyish, white-haired, portly man. "I suggest at the appropriate time, Mike, that the work of Doctor Spaniel be well and favorably publicized."

Quinn nodded, Yes, sir.

"Maybe we could prevail upon our friend the vice president to participate in the reburial ceremonies—if and when they come off," Krause added. "We'll work the Civil War angle on him."

Quinn moved his head to say yes to that possibility. The vice president was known for his interest in the Civil War.

Then Quinn said to Don, "Just for the record before we separate, Doctor Spaniel, a final question. Is there anything else—anything at all—that you think we should know about this situation before we proceed?"

For a half second, Don considered Reg's thesis about some kind of bad blood between Jim Allbritten and Fred Mackenzie. But even if that was true, it certainly wasn't relevant to what happened between their great-great-grandfathers.

Don said to Quinn, "No, sir, I have nothing to add."

But a few minutes later, he did tell Faye Lee Sutton. He had made a point to leave the room right behind her and then move up beside her as she clicked her heels in the direction of her office.

Under different circumstances, Don would have paused to admire the setting. They were walking through one of the high, wide corridors on the third floor of the Interior Department building at Eighteenth and C, Northwest, that Harold Ickes, FDR's interior secretary, had created during the New Deal. Don loved the story about how Ickes insisted on deciding most everything about the building, including the giant murals throughout that depicted not only the great life of animals outdoors but also the hard life of Americans—particularly Indians and blacks—everywhere.

"You probably should have told them," Faye Lee said, looking up at Don while not slowing her pace. She was about five foot six, nearly a foot shorter than Don. "Quinn will have your head if anything negative happens that the press can blame on the department and, by natural progression, on its most prominent and distinguished director."

"Maybe Womach's instincts were wrong," Don said. "Although I must confess I felt some unpleasantness between them, too."

Faye Lee, still moving, gave him a look that said, Why are you bringing this up with me?

Don responded with a smile that he hoped said, I wanted to say something that would grab your attention because I still think you are one terrific woman.

"What is it you history types say about those who ignore history being destined to repeat it?" Faye Lee asked as they arrived at the reception area for the offices of the general counsel.

"That's what we say," Don said, trying desperately to figure out what she meant, what she was getting at. Was she talking about violence on a long-ago battlefield repeating itself? Or was she speaking more personally about the history of their own relationship?

"What if we talked more about this over dinner tonight?" he said quickly. "We could go to the Old Ebbitt Grill or someplace else right here downtown—the Occidental or Red Sage?"

"Thanks, but no thanks," said Faye Lee, in a tone that was colder, flatter than the one she had used in the show-and-tell meeting.

Don was taken aback. "I must have misread your . . . well, your smiling approval just now."

"That was professional. I was applauding a job well done. Dinner is personal. When was it you said you were going to call me for a night out on the town—dinner, maybe a movie even? Wasn't that a year ago, maybe longer?"

Don said nothing.

"I'll call *you* tomorrow at your office at nine-fifteen to talk about the precise steps to be taken under all applicable federal laws and regulations to get those Antietam remains where they belong," said Faye Lee in the manner of a law book.

And she was gone, leaving behind no doubts about meanings or possibilities in cozy railway compartments.

10

As Don entered the office, a life-size oil painting jumped out at him. It was a portrait, from the chest up, of a young man in the uniform of a Union soldier. Don knew immediately that it was Roland F. Mackenzie—*the* Roland F. Mackenzie of the Eleventh Connecticut Volunteer Regiment.

Don had come to East Preston to meet with that man's great-great-grandson, Fred Mackenzie, and with Jim Allbritten, to begin carrying out the process Krause had approved. In separate phone calls, Don had told Mackenzie and Allbritten only that the Park Service investigation of the Burnside remains had concluded that both of their great-great-grandfathers were involved in the findings. He asked to see them in private, and, again separately, each invited him here to the Mackenzie Building law office of Fred Mackenzie for this joint meeting.

Don acknowledged Mackenzie's request to take a seat at a small conference table, but he walked first to an office window. He saw the town green where he had met these two men the first time. And there were the other buildings that ringed it, including the historical-society building down at the far end, next to the town hall. He looked straight ahead to the statue of the Civil War soldier. Visible beyond that was the church and the cemetery with the smaller statue with the same face that headed the grave marked as being that of Kenneth L. Allbritten.

Then he turned back to the office, which was huge, dark, and full of heavy furniture and law books and the delightful fragrances of must and time that went with them. He paid particular attention to a small waist-high table that had items Don recognized as from the Civil War era lying on it. There was a canteen and some letters and, most noticeable, a .44 Colt revolver similar to the one he had held at Milliken's sutlery. Was that a box of modern bullets lying next to it? If so, that meant the gun was probably from the special series of replicas that Colt made with up-to-date firing mechanisms.

But the real sight to behold, to fix on, was that portrait of Roland Mackenzie.

Based only on what he had read about him, Don had imagined Mackenzie as a harsh, rough man who spoke with force, who took charge. It was difficult to see that in the painting. His face was pink, probably the result of an overly zealous painter, and rather timid, gentle, mild—particularly for a man who had done what he had on that Antietam battlefield. But was it painted then, from life, when Mackenzie was, in fact, a young Union soldier?

"No, no," Fred Mackenzie said when Don asked, as he sat down at the table. "My grandfather—*his* grandson—had it done from old photographs in the early 1920s."

It was hard for Don to avoid looking at the man—the man he had come prepared to talk about, the man he had come, on behalf of the National Park Service, to accuse of being party to a murder.

Fred Mackenzie closely resembled his great-great-grandfather—or maybe Don wanted this man before him to be that earlier man of East Preston so much that he saw in him what he wanted. Fred Mackenzie was, to Don, Roland Mackenzie.

Jim Allbritten, on the other hand, did not have the same effect on Don. He saw no striking similarities between the photograph of Kenneth Allbritten and his great-great-grandson. With one exception: Jim Allbritten did have the build of a man who might have wrestled.

Marjorie Reston had, with the help of Nexis, searched the East Preston newspaper files and sketched some of the basics about these two men. So Don knew that Jim Allbritten had not been a wrestler. Instead, he had been the bulldozing football fullback who could always find a hole and yardage down the middle. While Fred Mackenzie was the fleet-footed halfback who could dash or swivel-hip past anybody around the end or on an open field. Together they took the East Preston Patriots to the state semifinals two out of the three years they played together in the backfield. They starred together, as well, in basketball and baseball, and they also, together, ran the student council and most everything else in every school they had ever attended—including Yale's undergraduate school. Both now had families of their own and practiced law—separately—in East Preston.

There was little in the news stories to support the intuition that there was bad trouble between the two. The only scent of anything was in the fact that reports about the side-by-side togetherness of Jim Allbritten and Fred Mackenzie, best of friends and of everything else, abruptly stopped while they were students at Yale Law School. And there was one recent story that portrayed them as "once best friends on and off the court, now most often opponents in and out of the courts."

They were now sitting side by side, fewer than two feet apart, across the table from Don. He looked in their faces for signs of dislike for each other. All he thought he saw were some tenseness and a desire to get on with it.

But Don had decided to go slowly. The question and answer about the Roland Mackenzie portrait served as a natural beginning.

"Mr. Mackenzie, Mr. Allbritten, I guess the two of you know the details of the battle of Antietam and the roles your great-great-grandfathers played?" he asked.

Without answering the question, Allbritten said Don should call him Jim. Mackenzie said he was Fred, and Don agreed to be Don.

"We know a lot but certainly not everything, Don," Fred said.

"And most certainly not as much as you, Don," Jim said.

Were they going to finish every sentence with "Don"? There was something much too labored, too prepared about this.

And before Don could say anything, Fred said: "We learned the most when we were seventeen years old."

"We were about to graduate from East Preston High School," Jim said.

"Somebody had the idea of turning our senior prom into a historical costume affair—everyone should come dressed in a way that 'reflected his or her own personal heritage,' " Fred said.

"My mother suggested a Civil War uniform for me, and when I mentioned it to Freddy he said that would be a perfect thing for him as well," Jim said.

Fred said: "It was a natural. There were few people around town who did not know of the Allbritten and Mackenzie Civil War connections. How could they miss it? As I'm sure you've noticed, Don, the names of Roland F. Mackenzie and Kenneth L. Allbritten, Union heroes, are everywhere."

Don mumbled, "I've noticed." He was taken aback by this most methodical, almost mechanical, performance going on before him. Something strange—and probably most important—was happening here.

Fred said that his mother made a call to a costume shop in Hartford to arrange for the rental of Union army outfits.

"But then I remembered the big trunk in the attic of our house. I had been told years ago that it was full of my great-great-grandfather's Civil War memorabilia and regalia."

Jim said he knew of nothing like that in his family from Kenneth L. Allbritten's short and tragic war life.

Picking up on each other's thoughts and sentences as if they had rehearsed, Jim Allbritten and Fred Mackenzie then told Don the story of how they found the trunk's key and headed for the attic.

They described the trunk as being about four feet long. It was made of wood covered with glued-on black canvas that was marked by many cracks, cuts, dents, water warping, and other signs of age and deterioration. There was no question about its exact age and heritage because painted in one-inch-high script in white paint on the center of the lid was the following:

Mackenzie
Eleventh Connecticut Volunteers
East Preston
–1861–

The key worked, and the lid opened easily.

The first thing that hit them, they said, was the strong smell of mildew and rotten leather that soared out.

The second was how little else besides that odor there was inside. Only a canteen, a leather belt with an elaborate military buckle, a leather knapsack, and a pair of worn-out boots. There were no uniforms—blouses or trousers—no caps, no swords or weapons. There was nothing that looked to Jim and Fred to be anything special—or wearable to a senior prom.

Then Fred opened the knapsack, the leather of which was dried out and cracked beyond repair. There was something down inside it. What looked like a rag was wrapped tight and held by a large rubber band around something small, rectangular. Not a book—too small for that.

"We figured we might as well see what it was," Fred said.

"Could be a million dollars in captured Confederate money or something," said Jim.

"I said it was possible, sure."

"But I told him no ancestor of *mine* would ever keep Confederate money after what the bastards did to Our Lieutenant," Jim said. He said *Our Lieutenant* was how some of the older Allbrittens still referred to Kenneth L. Allbritten, the family and town hero everyone believed was buried under the soldier's tombstone in Zion Cemetery.

They spoke quickly, almost as one, in alternating spurts.

"It was a small corduroy-covered box—about the size of an old tobacco tin—"

"It was sealed pretty tight from age—"

"Yeah, it took some doing to pry it open—"

"Inside was a folded piece of old paper—"

"Very old. It cracked as we began to open it—"

"But we were careful, and we got it unfolded—"

"There was a date at the top—"

"September something, 1910—"

"Written in large handwriting—"

"Like John Hancock's signature on the Declaration of Independence—"

"The words under it were also written as large—"

"They were faded, but we could still read them—"

"Barely—"

"There were only a few sentences, really—"

"He gave his name, Roland Mackenzie, and said he was sixty-seven years old—"

"He asked forgiveness for what he and somebody named Randolph did on a battlefield—"

"In Maryland—"

"In 1862—"

"He said he was driven to seek forgiveness, not out of remorse or guilt—"

"But because he believed in confession, absolution, and redemption—"

"He wanted to prosper well in the next life—"

"The only way to do it was to beg the forgiveness of his God—"

"Plus his fellow men and women of East Preston—"

"There was a big swirl of a signature, and that was it—"

"Not another word."

So. They had a whiff of something awful having happened on that battlefield 134 years ago? But they didn't know exactly what it was?

Don had barely drawn a breath while he listened to the remarkable presentation—the story these two men, no matter any personal problems between them, had clearly worked out to recite for him.

Don said nothing for several seconds. He thought about that knapsack, the one from which the strap came that was used to tie Kenneth Allbritten's hands behind him. Although no further confirmation was needed, there was also now in the record Mackenzie's plea for forgiveness—obviously for having committed the murder on the Antietam battlefield that Don had come to make his own recitation about for Jim Allbritten and Fred Mackenzie.

He looked back and forth between the portrait of Roland F.

Mackenzie and, out the window, the statues of the Civil War soldier.

Then he asked as matter-of-factly and calmly as he could manage: "Did you ever find out what it was Mr. Mackenzie—and the man Randolph—had done that required forgiveness?"

"No," said Jim.

"We asked the families and others around town, and nobody knew a thing," added Fred, ignoring Jim.

"So that was that—"

"We dropped it—"

"And we didn't think or talk about it again until we ran into you on the green, Don."

Ran into me? Ran after me, you mean.

"And then again when you called us on the phone to say your work was complete and asked to come meet with us."

They were, quite obviously, leaving out the time and energy they spent together getting their just-completed act in shape for this performance.

"Would you like to know *now* what the apology was all about?" Don Spaniel said to these two men of East Preston. "Do you want to know why he asked forgiveness?"

Fred and Jim looked at Don. Don had an instant, sweeping sense that both men, each in his own way, had come prepared to hear something terrible—to have their worst fears confirmed by the details of an event they had probably been unable to even imagine.

Jim Allbritten made the first gesture of response. He nodded at Don and said, "Certainly, tell us—that's why you're here. For chrissake, tell us."

"Then, it's now up to you, Mr. Mackenzie—Fred," Don said, moving into language he had worked out, over the phone, with

Faye Lee. "We at the Park Service have decided that if either of you have a problem with my telling you, then . . . well, we can move on to reburial matters."

"Reburial matters?" Jim barked. "What in the hell are you talking about?"

"The events and findings I would recount lead conclusively to the fact that those remains found near Burnside Bridge should be reburied here in East Preston."

"Tell your story, Doctor Spaniel," Fred Mackenzie said. The time of *Jim* and *Fred* and *Don* was over.

Don told them.

He cited the Randolph confession and his other research, and in the model of Colonel Doleman he even tried to raise the telling to its highest drama as he laid out the grim details of what happened to the men of the Eleventh Connecticut on that September 17 as they tried to take the Lower Bridge over the Antietam.

As they were forced back time after time.

As they saw their commanding colonel and then their captain and many of their fellow soldiers cut down by Confederate rifle and cannon fire from across the creek.

As they tried to see and breathe and live through it all.

As they stopped Lieutenant Kenneth L. Allbritten from leading them one more time down from the high ground into battle to what they thought was certain death for them and the others of the Eleventh Connecticut who remained alive.

As they grabbed him.

As they gagged him.

As they tied his hands behind him with a knapsack strap—most probably from the very knapsack found in Roland Mackenzie's old trunk.

As they grabbed Lieutenant Allbritten's Colt pistol—a .44 Police Colt.

As Roland F. Mackenzie and Albert Randolph together squeezed the trigger that shot a bullet through the base of Kenneth L. Allbritten's skull.

As they and the others buried Lieutenant Allbritten in a quickly dug grave on a hill just beyond the battlefield.

As they declared a dead messenger, his head blown to bits before their very eyes minutes before, to be Lieutenant Allbritten.

And as they agreed to lie forever about what had happened and what they had done.

The office of Fred Mackenzie, attorney-at-law, was absolutely silent. If there was a clock ticking somewhere, Don couldn't hear it. If there was noise from cars or people or rustling trees outside, Don couldn't hear them either. There were no telephones ringing, no radios or televisions playing. Time and life had been stopped by the story he had told.

Don saw huge tears in the brown eyes of Fred Mackenzie. "How sure are you of your facts?" he said softly, finally breaking the silence.

"The Randolph confession gives it an element of absolute certainty, Mr. Mackenzie."

There was rage in the blue eyes of Jim Allbritten.

"So the story about my great-great-grandfather, the one written down at the library and on the walls at town hall and retold every year at our Memorial Day ceremony on the green, is an absolute lie. He did not take a Rebel shot to the head?"

Don said that was so—that earlier story was not true.

"And all of that Mackenzie hero stuff that has been around here forever about Freddy's great-great-grandfather is a bunch of lies. Lies, lies, lies?"

"Wait a minute, Jimmy," said Fred Mackenzie, finally for the first time looking at Allbritten. "Hold on, keep your lid on. . . ."

And Jim and Fred, having moved back to being Jimmy and Freddy, were definitely no longer talking as one.

Jim said: "Lid on? Your great-great-grandfather murdered Our Lieutenant in cold blood! Did you hear that? I should have known."

"I heard, I heard," said Fred. "Calm down. It's awful—I am . . . well, stunned and so, so sorry. But let's not get carried away—"

"He was a traitor, a killer—a murderer. Plus a liar. The man so much in this town is named for. You come from the line of a cold-blooded lying killer. They tied up Our Lieutenant, shot him—executed him."

"They did it to save the lives of all the others, right, Doctor Spaniel?"

Don nodded and repeated what he had already told them, based on what Albert Randolph had written in his confession.

"It's still murder!" screamed Jim Allbritten, whose face was now beet red.

"No, it isn't," said Mackenzie, clearly trying hard to keep his voice and emotions modulated, under control. "People are often forced by circumstances of war to commit acts of brutality they would never do under normal circumstances—"

"Spoken like the goddamn liar that you are."

"Spoken only as the sad great-great-grandson that I am—you bastard."

Jim Allbritten sprang to his feet. "*Bastard*. You know about bastards, don't you?"

Here now it comes? A piece of more recent history involving these two descendants of Kenneth Allbritten and Roland Mackenzie?

But Fred Mackenzie said nothing, and Jim Allbritten went to the window. "I feel like taking some sledgehammers and chisels and doing some editing on a few buildings and streets and monuments in this town. Eliminate some naming or at least change everything to 'Roland F. Mackenzie, traitorous cold-blooded lying killer.' "

Fred, his eyes staring at the back of Jim said, "All of this happened more than one hundred and thirty years ago, Jimmy. We're civilized people. We're not Bosnians or Serbs or the IRA or the Protestants of Northern Ireland. We move on, we don't carry on our ancestors' hates. . . ."

Jim turned back toward Don and Fred. In four strides, he was in front of the large painting of Roland F. Mackenzie in his Civil War uniform. He grabbed it from the wall and flung it toward Fred's display table, scattering the .44 Colt and the other items in all directions.

Then he bolted out of the office, slamming the door hard behind him.

"Don't worry about him, Doctor Spaniel," said Fred Mackenzie to Don after a few seconds of silence. "He blows up, and then he always calms down. He's been doing it since he took his first called strike in a baseball game."

Don, though understanding, was truly shaken by the intensity of Jim Allbritten's anger. He could only take Fred Mackenzie's word that here was a man who always calmed down. Thus far, he had seen no such signs.

"So who exactly is under that statue over there?" asked Fred Mackenzie, now steady on his feet, pointing toward Zion Cemetery, across the green.

Don, now also standing, said he and his researchers believed it was a Union officer from Illinois.

It was an answer that appeared to be of no importance to Mackenzie. "The bottom line is Kenneth Allbritten had to die that day so many others could live," he said, his voice faltering. "That is so, is it not, Doctor Spaniel?"

"That's obviously what your great-great-grandfather and the others believed, sir, yes."

"What do *you* believe?"

Don's reflex answer was no. Nobody has the right to make such a decision about another man's life.

What he said to Mackenzie was, "I'm not qualified to pass such judgments."

"I am fully qualified by birth and blood to do so. I know my great-great-grandfather did the right thing. He clearly believed Allbritten was out of his mind and was going to lead the rest of them to slaughter. He took action. And he moved on from the experience to a full and fruitful life here in East Preston. End of story."

Don chose not to react. He certainly wasn't going to get into an argument.

Mackenzie accepted the silence and then asked, "What now? What is it exactly that you and your superiors in the federal government want to do?" An unmistakable message of hostility was coming from Roland Mackenzie's great-great-grandson.

First, Don said, the National Park Service, in cooperation with the Department of Defense and others, stood ready to exhume the remains under the statue and rebury them wherever the other lieutenant's descendants desire. Then, the real remains of Lieutenant Allbritten would be interred here in East Preston. Everything could be done with full and appropriate military honors, if so desired. The vice president of the United States might even come to the ceremony.

"I'd love it if the vice president came, because I'm a Democrat," Mackenzie said, but with a tinge of impatience, annoyance. "The reburial issue is Jimmy's, not mine—did you notice, by the way, how we reverted to calling each other by our kid names?"

Don acknowledged with a nod that he had noticed.

"What I will not tolerate, Doctor Spaniel, is anything that results in the name and memory of my great-great-grandfather being besmirched," Mackenzie continued. His voice rose in velocity and pitch. "What business is it of the federal government's to dig—literally and otherwise—into such matters of personal history anyhow?"

Don ignored the last point and said, "The remains relocation could be done without the battlefield story being made public, if that's what you want, Mr. Mackenzie." There, he'd done it. Don had offered the deal—again in words he and Faye Lee had composed. Silence and the vice president in exchange for an exhumation and reburial.

"Are you certain about that?"

"Yes. Obviously, there are now others who also know about this, though."

"Jimmy Allbritten, you mean?"

Don nodded.

"Anyone else?"

"No one who could not be persuaded to remain silent about the story." Neither Reg nor Ms. Fentress, of course, would require any persuasion. He had in mind the people sitting around that table at the Interior Department show-and-tell meeting.

"Jimmy can also be persuaded," Mackenzie said. "He will come to his senses, and this project of yours will soon have a happy ending."

Fred Mackenzie stopped talking. He looked away from Don,

first at his own hands folded down in front of him and then out the window.

Then he said right at Don: "There will be a reburial, but there will be no murder story on the front page of our or any other newspaper. Now, if you'll excuse me, I have other appointments."

Don saw flash in the eyes of Fred Mackenzie a look of directed purpose that no doubt resembled that of his great-great-grandfather as he went about the business of killing and burying Kenneth Allbritten on September 17, 1862.

And, as he took one last look at Roland F. Mackenzie's pink-faced portrait still there on the floor, Don shivered with the feeling that the demons Ms. Fentress had warned about may have been awakened here in East Preston, Connecticut.

But the shivers were soon replaced by a consuming feeling of satisfaction. Yes, he had unleashed on two men of the present some deeply jarring emotions and passions from the past.

Exactly. So be it. Precisely. And amen.

History requires Jim Allbritten to deal with the fact that his great-great-grandfather was murdered by his friends on a field of battle.

As it requires Fred Mackenzie to accept the reality of—and, yes, maybe even some responsibility for—his great-great-grandfather being one of the murderers.

11

Young Doctor Spaniel, as the colonel called him, hadn't given much thought to how he would be dispatched to his maker. Until now. Until this afternoon as he sat in the second row of the Christ Reformed Church in Sharpsburg, Maryland.

This is it. When my time comes, this is the kind and style and sound and feel of the funeral I want. I will go the same way as Colonel Gary Doleman. I may not deserve to, but I want to.

The colonel had passed away in his sleep two nights before. Mrs. Doleman had said that as a precaution she had weeks earlier made it a point to give her dying husband a vigorous goodnight kiss every night, just in case he slipped away while he slept. As a result, she had said her good-byes without knowing for sure it would be this particular night.

This church was a special place for the colonel because it had been used as a field hospital for Union—mostly Connecticut—wounded on September 17, 1862. It was a small, plain, redbrick structure with a single-aisle sanctuary filled with little more than a few crosses, framed paintings of Jesus, and hard dark-wood pews for some two hundred people. Most every space was filled with mourners this morning. Don assumed the church's basic appearance, inside and out, had not changed much since that awful day young men were carried here so they could live but mostly died or, at the very least, were left without an arm or leg. The major additions to the church were probably only the four stained-glass windows that were donated in the 1890s by members of the three Connecticut regiments that had been at Antietam.

The one for the Eleventh was a small vertical piece of glass in the vestibule—swords, bullets, cannon, bayonets, and rifles on one side, farming tools such as a hoe and a rake on the other.

Windows. Don recalled from his Carlisle readings that a deep hole had been dug just outside a window of this church—probably the one behind the pulpit—so the surgeons could drop the arms and legs they amputated directly into a pit and out of sight.

Don looked up at that window, and, with his imagination, he saw that they were working right now on a particular young man with a large mustache, his tattered blue uniform covered in blood. He was being held down on a table by two other soldiers, also with mustaches. A surgeon, a man with a long black beard as well as mustache and whose white coat was stained with a mixture of fresh and caked blood, held a huge handsaw over the soldier's right leg just below the groin.

"Sorry, dear lad of Connecticut, but this must be done," said the surgeon, who was at least twice the age of his patient.

The doctor sawed harshly forward and then backward. Once, twice—again. And again. It eventually became a soft, rhythmic movement not unlike that of a skilled baker slicing a loaf of freshly baked bread.

Blood spurted, a tiny geyser, straight up onto the doctor's coat and all over the two soldiers. The handsaw must have cut a major artery.

There was a scraping, gnawing sound as the blade moved on down, struck, and then began a slow passage through bone.

The overriding noise was that coming out of the young soldier's mouth. It was a steady, horrific, thundering scream of no words, only a sound resembling the highest, loudest, most sour blare of a trumpet. Or of an animal dying?

Don remembered Joseph Campbell's Newberne hospital account.

He also recalled, from his reading, the story of a Sharpsburg girl of twelve who wrote in her diary twenty years later that she had never closed her eyes to sleep since without hearing the piercing, wrenching shrieks of those young soldiers having their limbs sawed off in the churches on Main Street.

Enough. Enough remembering. And imagining.

Back in the real world of this memorial service for the colonel, the sounds were words of testimony, honor, and remembrance. The first speaker was Colonel Doleman's daughter, Rachel, a robust woman of fifty-plus who was a high school girls-basketball coach in Delaware. This morning, she was dressed in a dark blue pantsuit as she spoke from the pulpit about her father.

"There's something exquisitely different about having a father who spent most of his waking—sleeping, too, for all I know—moments caught square in the middle of the chaos and suffering and horror and heroism of a war fought many—he would say 'scores'—of years ago. When my friends would ask me what my father did for a living, I was tempted to whistle some ditty of death and proclaim that he lived the Civil War. He lived the battle of Antietam. That's what my father did for his living—for his existence. He lived it so that he could know and understand the young men who died in this church, in this town, and on its battlefield. It was a full life, a rewarding life. We could all be so lucky."

Rachel Doleman Barton spoke with a deep firmness of voice

that was a feminine near-replica of the colonel's. Don was struck also by the simple fact that she could speak at her father's funeral without breaking down. He couldn't imagine doing such a thing for his mother or father. He was too emotional—too sentimental.

There were two other speakers. A young woman history professor at Shepherd College talked about Gary Doleman's inspiring passion and dedication. An archivist at Carlisle—one who had helped Don, in fact—compared the colonel to the best and most famous of the military historians. "Colonel Doleman did not write books about what he knew, he spoke volumes," said the archivist. He was a trim, bald man in his late sixties who had won the Bronze Star and Purple Heart as an army intelligence officer in Korea.

Then, everyone, accompanied by only a piano that was being played somewhere in the back, sang "The Battle Hymn of the Republic." There were no silent voices or dry eyes among the mourners. Don was fighting back sobs. He could see and feel Abraham Lincoln and the rolling cannon and marching troops and shuffling wounded and crying families that he always associated with the sounds of that song of war.

A middle-aged preacher in a black suit and with close-cropped blond hair read something from the Bible about the need to remember what he called "the battlers for good and history." When he finished several—joined by Don—yelled out, "Amen!"

It was the first time in the thirty-seven years of Don Spaniel's life that he spontaneously shouted anything in a church—or, for that matter, any other public place.

The closing moments that followed brought him to a state of mind far beyond shouting.

To the one-stick beat of a drum, down the center aisle of the church came two men in uniform. One, on the left, was in the gray of the Confederate army, the other in Union blue. Both were moving slowly from their obvious wounds, their faces drawn in pain. The Yank was on crutches that appeared to be made from tree limbs. His left foot and leg were bandaged with blood-soaked white cloth that showed below the end of his trousers. His face was bruised, and there was another bandage around his head, under his kepi. The Reb soldier was bareheaded and barefoot. The right side of his face was marked by a half-inch-wide bloody scar from his hairline to below his chin, and he walked with the help of a makeshift cane in his left hand. His right arm was in a sling of cloth that was soiled by dirt and greenish-brown filth.

For a split second Don thought he had again been taken over by his imagination. But no. *This is real. That's the Civil War shop man! The Reb soldier is that guy Milliken—the Thaddeus Farm relic hunter.*

Milliken and his fellow reenactor for the Union went to the front of the church, to the bottom of the three steps that led up the pulpit, stopped, and then, with great effort, turned around to face the crowd, the mourners.

Each soldier moved to make room between them for Rachel Doleman Barton and the preacher, who came down from the stage and the pulpit.

Rachel held a brown clay urn in her hands in front of her.

From the back of the church came the muted blare of a real trumpet. "Taps." To Don, the most emotively mournful sound man and music ever created.

Don stayed in the church, in his pew, until the family and the other mourners had departed—and until Rachel Doleman Barton returned. That had been their arrangement.

"My mother and I truly appreciate your willingness to do

this," she said now, handing Don the clay urn. Rachel was at least five foot eleven and very much resembled her father, not only in voice but in presence and bearing. Don figured she was a great coach.

"It's an honor," said Don, accepting the urn.

When he left the church a few minutes later, he drove first to Milliken's store two blocks away.

A handmade sign on the front door said the store was closed for the afternoon in honor of Colonel Gary Doleman, "an Antietam Hero." But Don, going up some outside stairs, found Henry Milliken in a second-floor apartment, where he lived. He was still wearing the remnants of his reenacted life as a severely wounded Confederate soldier.

Don praised the realism of Milliken's funeral performance. "You seemed as if you had really become that soldier," said Don.

"I had, that's the point. I was playing a real guy from the Twentieth Georgia who had those exact wounds that I had—"

Don interrupted. "You offered to loan me some stuff—a uniform coat and hat—if I ever needed it," Don said to him.

Milliken confirmed the offer still stood and, after looking hard at Don's face, added, "You all right, Doctor Spaniel?"

Don nodded.

"You look like you've just seen a ghost or something. You and the colonel, I take it, must have been real close. Can I get you something to drink? A beer? Coffee or something else hot?"

Don said nothing, and Milliken shrugged but didn't press for a response to any of the questions. His face was now clean of makeup blood and dirt, but he was still dressed in the butternut trousers of a Rebel soldier and a long-sleeved white undershirt.

Milliken led Don down a flight of inside stairs and into the dark store and the sutlery.

After turning on the light, Milliken went to the rack and pulled out the forty-two long coat of a Union lieutenant and, from overhead, selected a matching officer's kepi. "You going to do a little reenacting of your own, doctor, is that it? What's up?"

Don put on the coat and hat—he had taken off his fedora in the car—and said he would return the gear in an hour or so.

"Take your time, Doctor Spaniel. You want me to go with you? I can get back in my rig—without the wounds—in a second and go and do whatever you've got in mind. In any fight two soldiers are always better than one."

Don declined the offer. And he had one more request. "The Colt pistol. Could I borrow that, too?"

Milliken hesitated. "You up on how to load and fire one of those things? They can shoot real cap-and-ball bullets or just make a noise and some smoke. But either way, they're deadly. That black powder can be dangerous if you're not real careful."

"I don't want to fire it," said Don, "only carry it."

Milliken went again to his locked armory closet and retrieved the replica Colt .44 and handed it to Don, handle first.

Raising the pistol to his hat rim in the motion of a salute, Don said, "Thank you, sir."

"Not proper for you to say 'sir' to me," said Milliken, moving his heels together and his shoulders back. "Right now, I'm a sergeant in the Confederate army, sir, only an enlisted man. You're an officer, a Union lieutenant."

On the way out, Don paused momentarily in front of a full-length mirror on a door, adjusting his kepi and the pistol, which he had thrust into his uniform belt.

Yes, sergeant. Right now, I'm a Union lieutenant.

———

Don parked the car in a small twelve-car lot up behind what had been the Confederate high ground. It overlooked the bridge and the opposite side, the Union side, from where he and the colonel had begun their dramatic tour of the battlefield a few weeks ago. No other cars were there, which had been his expectation this late in the afternoon, it being already after four o'clock, just an hour to closing.

Holding the urn in both hands in front of him, he walked down and around the concrete steps behind a row of what had been the rifle pits of the Twentieth Georgia. The bridge down below was again in full view to Don as it had been to the Confederates—as it had been to him and Colonel Doleman when they came over to this side. He took the blacktop path marked "Burnside Bridge Walk" down from the high ground toward the bridge.

There at the west end, the Confederate end of the bridge, Don paused and had no trouble again imagining it, per the colonel's description, filled with Union soldiers, four or five abreast, running toward him, leaping over the bodies of their fallen comrades, slipping on the blood of their fallen comrades. . . .

He turned to his right to follow a trail for a few yards, stopping in the place the colonel had identified as the hallowed ground. This was where Captain John Griswold of Lyme, Connecticut, had, after leading Albert Randolph and a few others into the Antietam, died his hero's death.

Don, his blue-jacketed chest forward and his shoulders back, rigidly held the urn out in front of him. He longed for the sound of "Taps."

He said out loud to no one—to everyone: "I come here now with the ashes of Gary Wayne Doleman, Colonel, U.S. Army, Retired, to make them part of the soil that meant so much to him and is where they belong, here with those of the men who died here on September 17, 1862. May *they* rest in peace, and may he rest with them now and forever more. Amen."

Don removed the lid from the urn. Then, with both hands, as if fertilizing a garden, he gently sprinkled the ashes onto the ground.

And he tossed the urn and its lid into the running water of the Antietam.

Back at the bridge, instead of turning left back up the pathway and steps to the parking lot, he went to his right across the bridge.

He was filled with a sudden, consuming urge to do something more while he was here.

On the other side, the Union side, he made another right, walking by the spot on the bank of the creek where Captain Griswold, followed by Albert Randolph and others, had entered the water. Don moved closer to the edge. The water was clear. He could see the bottom, and he could see back to the opposite side, where he had just spread Colonel Doleman's ashes.

With nothing firm in mind, he moved on, following what had been the road on September 17, 1862. Now it was a ten-yard wide path, bordered on the right by the creek, on the left by the wooden fence. He cut through the opening in the fence and walked twenty yards across and up the rise to the Eleventh Connecticut memorial and tablet.

There again was the gray monument, with the small bronze diorama of the battle for the bridge in the center.

He read, again out loud, the names of the dead. He began quietly, but by the time he neared the end of the list, his voice had reached an emotional pitch.

"Colonel Henry Kingsbury . . . Captain John Griswold . . . Lieutenant Kenneth L. Allbritten . . . Christian Steinmetz . . . William Halbfass . . . First Sergeant J. R. Read . . . Corporal G. R. Crane . . . Edward Deming . . . Lewis Aiken . . . Alvin Flint, Junior . . . Henry Rising . . . First Sergeant Hiram C. Roberts . . . Corporal Theodore S. Bates . . . Benjamin J. Beech . . . William F. Cogswell . . . Theodore Parrett . . . George I. Wilson . . . Clinton Fessington . . . David Tarbox . . . Fenimore Weeks . . . Frank Chaffee . . . George H. Heflin . . . William H. Hitchcock . . . Corporal David M. Ford . . . Corporal John C. Hallwell . . . Corporal Orville P. Armstrong . . . Avis Batty . . . William H. Hall . . . Thomas Lawson . . . Charles H. Morris . . . Samuel C. Rogers . . . Asa W. Rouse . . . John H. Walker . . . James Morgan . . . John Murray . . . Albert Todd . . . First Sergeant George E. Bailey . . . Henry W. Davis . . . Williams H. Houghton . . . William Lane . . ."

Don then raised a hand to the bill of his Union officer's kepi and almost shouted: "And Colonel Gary Wayne Doleman!"

It occurred to him that he probably should feel like some kind of fool, saluting and yelling the colonel's name toward the battlefield and the Antietam. But he had seldom felt less a fool.

The ravine. Why not take a look? There was no path, only brambles and sticky bushes and small trees and rock outcroppings. He made his way carefully and slowly through it to the very end, suffering a few pricks in his hands and legs from stickers on branches.

He found the spot where the murder must have happened.

In silence, he created—imagined—the scene.

There was terrifying noise from the guns and the wounded. An officer comes up to Lieutenant Allbritten, now in charge by default, of a company of men he has known all his life. The officer delivers the order. . . .

What direction did he come from? Where did he tie up his horse?

The Confederate cannon round. From out of the trees, from on high it comes. . . .

Did they hear it coming? What did a round from a Confederate cannon sound like on its way to a target? Did it whine? Did it buzz? Did it sing?

The shot crashes into the officer. It blows his face and the rest of his head into many pieces. . . .

Don, as he thought of it, automatically looked down and around. Was it remotely possible there might still be any pieces of that man's cranium here?

Lieutenant Allbritten, sickened by the other man's awful death and determined to carry on, screams orders to Albert Randolph, Roland T. Mackenzie, and the others. . . .

Had it made him insane? Would it have been crazy to try again to take that bridge? Were Mackenzie and Randolph and the others justified in thinking so at that superheated moment?

There's a struggle, they tie him up and gag him, and then Mackenzie and Randolph shoot him through the back of his head with his own pistol. . . .

They carry Allbritten's body from here, where he was shot, to over there. . . .

Obsessed, Don searched the ground frantically and then the gulley farther on, and then past it across the blacktop road to the high ground where the remains of Kenneth L. Allbritten had been found. Don could see the grave site through the trees, up there, less than fifty yards away.

He stood still and silent for several moments.

Then, compelled to do something else, he moved toward the high ground.

Within minutes, he was at the place on the hillside where he had felt the need to promise an unknown Union soldier that he would neither disturb his peace nor do him harm.

The wire stakes, red-flag markers, trowels, metal detectors, and the other tools and signs of archeology were gone. The dirt was back in its place, beginning again a natural process that might take another 134 years for the now empty battlefield grave of Lieutenant Kenneth Leonard Allbritten to disappear again under a cover of grass and weeds and brush.

Don Spaniel, Union lieutenant, turned to face in the direction of the bridge.

There it was, down there through the trees, some two hundred yards away, its peaceful and pastoral appearance still belying its bloody history.

Don looked to make sure that the eight buttons of the dark blue coat were properly buttoned. He used his left hand to push the Union officer's hat down on his head a bit farther—to make the fit tighter.

Then, with his right hand, he raised the pistol high over his head and shouted:

"Forward! Onward, Eleventh! Double-quick!"

And he took off running toward the bridge.

He heard the roar of cannon and musket fire as he crossed the road and dashed through a Park Service fence onto the battlefield and onto the next, smaller hill.

He raced at full speed past the Eleventh Connecticut's marble monument and blue metal tablet.

"Go! Eleventh!" he screamed. "Go! Go! Onward!"

Now he was out of the trees, exposed. He saw the flashes from Reb guns on the bluffs across the Antietam and felt the wind from their minié balls as he ran a zigzag path toward the wooden fence that paralleled the Antietam. He heard screams and smelled powder exploding.

At the fence, he cut right and ran alongside the creek toward the bridge.

Men in blue were falling, dying, yelling, wailing in front of him, behind him, on both sides of him.

"This time! This time, Eleventh, we'll take it! Onward!"

He barely slowed down as he streaked onto the bridge.

"Charge! Go, Eleventh! Go!"

Four strides, barely a third of the way across, his right foot slipped out from under him.

The blood! He had forgotten about the blood on the bridge!

He dropped the pistol and reached out to break his fall.

His forehead crashed against the top of the railing, sending the kepi flying.

Piercing pain shot through the top of his head as he fell, sprawling backward.

His eyes felt heavy.

"Hey, Doctor Spaniel!"

It was a familiar voice. A man's voice. *Who is he? Where am I? What happened to my troops? Did they all fall, too?*

Don opened his eyes into the face of a Confederate soldier.

"You OK, Doctor Spaniel?" asked Henry Milliken.

The relic hunter. Mr. Antietam Memories. The wounded Reb at the church.

"I got worried about you after you left the shop. I thought this might be where you were headed."

I am not unconscious.

"I don't think, lieutenant, sir, that the surgeons will see the need to amputate anything."

I couldn't get the Eleventh across the bridge!

"I don't think they'll saw off your head, to be really specific, which is the best news. Looks like you've got a small cut there, it's bleeding a bit, but nothing serious."

I am not unconscious. My cranium hurts, but it's getting better.

In slow motion, Don shook his head a few times and blinked his eyes and sat up.

Henry Milliken, down on his knees with Don, gave a hand of steadying support. Don now saw that Milliken was in the full uniform of a Confederate sergeant, and he was holding a long rifle down by his side.

"That was quite a run you made down from the trees," Milliken said. "I had you in my sights all the way from the battle pits up there. I could have easily picked you off—just like it was that day."

"I didn't make it across the bridge."

"The Eleventh didn't, you can't," said Milliken, with a gospel firmness. "You can't reenact it any other way than the way it happened."

Don put his right hand to his forehead. Yes, there was a cut, there was some blood—not much. But it wasn't anything to worry about. A Band-Aid would be all that's required.

Milliken was still talking. "If the Eleventh had gotten across the bridge, then McClellan would have probably defeated Lee here, and the war would have ended nearly three years earlier that it actually did. There'd have been no Gettysburg, no Fredericksburg, no Petersburg, no Appomattox. . . ."

Don knew all of that. With Milliken's help, he stood up. No pain. No breaks of bones or other trauma. No dizziness, no unsteadiness.

"Sorry about your gear," he said, unbuttoning the blue coat of a Union lieutenant. "I'll pay to have this coat cleaned and pressed."

"No, no. My wife and I do all of that kind of thing the old-fashioned way right there at the place. By hand, by brush, no chemicals, no liquids. Nothing seems to be damaged—no tears, rips. The kepi and the pistol came through OK, too."

Don thanked Henry Milliken for the use of the equipment and for coming to his aid. He said he was fine now and would walk up to where he had parked his car and drive back to Washington.

His head was clearing.

"Why don't you come to the house with me now for a bite or sip of something first—and we'll give that cut a good cleaning and dressing," said Milliken. "You probably don't need to get out on the road driving for a while anyhow."

Don declined the invitation.

"It really wasn't your fault you didn't get over the bridge," Milliken said.

Don, no longer a Union lieutenant, gave a half salute to this man dressed as a Confederate sergeant.

Milliken returned the salute in a military manner.

"This was the way it was supposed to end," he said.

12

There they were.

Don had heard their sounds first. From his seat on a stage erected at the church and cemetery side of the green, he listened to the slow, soft beat and roll of the drums, the clicking of heels on the old brick of Allbritten Street.

There now, where the street dead-ended from the south into the green, emerged the soldiers in their dress blue uniforms and white gloves, their glistening rifles and swords and buttons and buckles and belts and shoes.

They were twenty officers and men of the U.S. Army's Old Guard, the troops who guard the Tomb of the Unknowns and perform other ceremonial duties at Arlington National Cemetery in Washington.

Today, in the warm sunshine of this September 17, their duty was to bury Kenneth L. Allbritten.

His remains followed the soldiers in a black Cadillac hearse. The vehicle came through the street opening, turned, and stopped behind the soldiers in front of the town hall and the historical-society museum.

Eight soldiers, moving as one, went to the rear of the hearse and slid out a gray steel casket, draped in an American flag.

The drumming stopped.

And Don, seventy-five yards away, was hit by a sudden rush of tears to his eyes.

"Present arms!" shouted an army captain. The honor guard dipped their flags, and the other soldiers saluted with hands, swords, or rifles.

Then they turned in a series of precise movements. The drums rolled, and the eight soldiers, four to a side, moved with the casket across the green. They marched, slowly and deliberately, down a wide center aisle between several hundred folding chairs. All of the seats were taken, and many more people were standing in the back and on both sides.

Don was on the stage at the end of the aisle—the soldiers' destination—that was decorated with red, white, and blue streamers and old-fashioned American eagles and flags. He was there as a special guest among the dignitaries, including the vice president of the United States, who would participate in the ceremony.

Don had imagined what this occasion, this reburial of Kenneth Allbritten, might be like. Even now, as it was only beginning, he was overcome by its moving majesty. The officials of the town of East Preston, working with a variety of people from the federal government, had gotten it absolutely right.

The soldiers, still to no sound except the *bang-roll-bang* of the drums, arrived at the foot of the stage.

Then, in another series of sharp, military moves, they placed the casket on a long table, stepped back, saluted smartly, and marched off to one side.

Doris Michelle Haynes, the mayor of the town, went to a podium that was completely draped with flowers. Don had met her earlier. She was an all-business attractive redheaded woman of forty-five or so. She said into a microphone: "We of East Preston are in a place of history, and we are making more of it today. Would you please join in the singing of our national anthem."

All but the soldiers joined in the singing of "The Star-Spangled Banner." The voices, low and soft as the drums, mixed well and floated beautifully out from the crowd. Don couldn't remember a time he had ever heard it sung better or more movingly.

The mayor spoke again: "I want to extend a welcome to the vice president and to everyone on behalf of our citizens and our ancestors, who came before us and prepared for us this wonderful place in the hills to live in, nurture, and prosper in."

This place in the hills, it seemed to Don, was made even more sparkling this particular September day, not only by the welcoming sunshine but also by the sky that was a perfect blue and the temperature that was a perfect seventy-five degrees.

Jim Allbritten spoke next. He seemed edgy, distraught—angry. Don was particularly struck by how worn down Allbritten appeared, compared to the earlier times he had been with him, particularly just four weeks ago at Fred Mackenzie's office. His blue eyes had red circles around them and bags underneath them, and his stocky body appeared to have sagged considerably, as if weighted down by something large and heavy.

Apparently, there had been no calming down. But, Don thought, why shouldn't he be in a state of unrelenting anger over what Mackenzie and Randolph and the others did to his great-great-grandfather? Particularly right now, on this day. It must—*must*—run through his ancestral blood and soul!

Don felt Allbritten's anger. It raced through him. His eyes went dry. There was warmth in his face, a twitching in both of his forearms.

In a shaking voice, Jim Allbritten thanked everyone for coming today to help us "honor my loved one, Kenneth L. Allbritten."

Don suddenly feared what Allbritten might say next. The agreement Faye Lee Sutton worked out formally called for placing Kenneth L. Allbritten in his proper grave in East Preston but without making public the battlefield-murder story. The informal understanding was that everyone involved, including Jim Allbritten, would simply say the chaos on that Antietam battlefield at the end of the day led to the bodies of two Union officers getting mixed up.

But was Allbritten now, right before everyone, going to blow away that cover story? Faye Lee had told Don—again, always, in a phone call—that she felt Allbritten agreed to the silence only because he didn't want to do anything to distract from the reburial ceremony.

"I am particularly grateful to the vice president of the United States for being here today," said Allbritten. "Ladies and gentlemen, the vice president."

The crowd stood and applauded as Jim Allbritten returned to his seat. So, Don thought, Jim Allbritten's manner and appearance had sent out a false alarm. Whatever the state of his emotions at these moments, he would contain his outrage—he would honor the agreement.

Don felt relief. Then, unexpectedly, a sense of disappointment—and annoyance—swept through him.

The vice president moved to the microphone. He was a fifty-two-year-old man of imposing stature and prematurely silver hair. And the first thing he did was to ask Don to stand.

Don knew this was going to happen. He was ready. His main regret was that he had not thought to ask his mother and father to come this morning. He had urged Faye Lee Sutton to be present, but she declined with only a shade more of a personal touch than she probably used in dismissing a telemarketer. That had ended it, once and for all. Don would move on with his romantic sights and imagination. There was still plenty of time. . . .

"This young man works for you, the taxpayers of America," said the vice president. "On the next occasion when you hear someone speak of the worthless bureaucrats in Washington, remember the face and work of this young man. Remember Doctor Don Spaniel of the National Park Service. Remember what he did to bring the long-lost remains of your young man back home to you today."

The crowd knew what the stranger from Washington had done because the story had been in the town's newspaper. Everyone stood and applauded.

Don rose to his feet and acknowledged the attention and honor with a wave. He had never felt better in his life. *Who in the hell needs Faye Lee Sutton?*

The vice president spoke generally of the legacies of the Civil War and then went to the heart of what he had come to say today. He explained the sounds of a bugle and rifles that would soon be heard over the remains of Kenneth Allbritten. "Taps," the great musical tribute to the end of a soldier's life, was composed by a Union army general in 1862. The firing of three rifle volleys was a custom that came into being during earlier wars when armies often halted hostilities to clear the battlefield of their respective dead. Each fired three volleys when the clearing was done—signaling that the battle, the killing, and the maiming could resume.

The vice president, intentionally or not, went on to give some credence to the cover story. He said: "On the bloodiest day of U.S. military history—September 17, 1862—at Burnside Bridge on the banks of the Antietam, there was no time for volleys, for 'Taps'—for formal burials and ceremonies. There was horrendous confusion on that horrendous battlefield on that horrendous day. That confusion is now over. It ends now on this day, at this moment, on this September 17, one hundred and thirty-four years later. We have all come here to fire delayed volleys and blow delayed bugle calls and say delayed prayers."

The vice president, Don, and the others on the stage then walked down the steps and formed a two-abreast file behind the Old Guard soldiers.

There was again the slow drumbeat and the click of heels and metal.

The casket, in the hands once more of eight soldiers, joined the procession behind the platform dignitaries. A three-quarter-size statue of a Civil War soldier on a tombstone was visible. That was the one Don and Reg had seen when they parked their car at the cemetery on that first visit to East Preston.

The grave in front of the tombstone was now open. Freshly spaded dirt was neatly banked on both sides.

Seven soldiers with rifles stood off to one side about twenty yards away.

The casket was brought to the grave and set down across the top on several large dark blue straps.

The army captain commanded: "Firing party . . . atten-hut!"

The seven soldiers came to attention with their rifles.

"Ready . . ."

The soldiers raised their rifles to their right shoulders.

"Aim . . ."

The soldiers sighted the rifles at an angle toward the perfect sky.

"Fire!"

The seven rifles fired as one. Wham!

The captain repeated the commands. And the soldiers fired again.

And again, through it all a third time.

An army bugler, from a position out of sight among the tombstones, blew "Taps." From there, it came as a sound of inclusion, as if his moving, echoing *da-da-daa*s were for everyone buried here, for everyone gathered here.

Once again, Don felt his emotions rising. Was it simply the sounds and sights of this moving ceremony? Or was it the sympathy with Jim Allbritten's frustrations burning inside him?

The eight soldiers at the casket stepped forward and took the edges of the flag. They lifted it up to waist level, pulled it taut, and began folding it. It took thirty folds and a couple of silent minutes to complete the task.

The captain in charge of the detail then delivered the flag to Jim Allbritten, who was standing at the foot of the grave with the vice president. Don thought for a second Jim Allbritten might not take the flag. His face was screwed up and crimson. He was clearly struggling to control himself.

Allbritten accepted the flag with both hands, and the captain saluted, stepped back, and marched his casket team away from the grave site.

An Episcopal priest in a bright purple robe moved in. He was thin, olive-skinned, black-haired, and slightly affected—in that kind of wanna-be Brit way favored by the occasional philosophy major Don met at UVA. Don guessed the man's age at around forty.

The priest said a prayer: "O God, whose mercies cannot be numbered: Accept our prayers on behalf of thy servant who made the ultimate sacrifice for his country, his people, and his beliefs. We stand here because he stood there on the banks of the Antietam. Grant him an entrance into the land of light and joy, in the fellowship of the saints, through Jesus Christ the Son, our Lord, who liveth and reigneth with thee and the Holy Spirit, One God, now and forever. Amen."

It was over. Four months after his remains were found by two relic hunters, Lieutenant Kenneth L. Allbritten of the Eleventh Connecticut Volunteers was now at proper rest.

Yes, rest for him, thought Don. *But what about his great-great-grandson? He's not at rest!*

Don glanced around and saw that most of the people here were crying over this man who had died 134 years ago. *How remarkable,* he thought. *How absolutely wonderful.*

The vice president, unapologetic for his well-publicized tendency to tear up, wiped his eyes slowly with a handkerchief and said his good-byes to the mayor and others. When he got to Don he`said, "I meant what I said about you. Congratulations on a job well done for the American people and for history, Doctor Spaniel."

"History creates its own imperatives," Don said. He said it as smartly, sternly as he could. "Thank you, sir."

"How are you coming on the other remains, those that used to be here?" the vice president asked. "Am I going to have another reburial ceremony to attend soon?"

Don told the vice president that they had now identified the first remains as being those of Lieutenant Richard Allen Rhodes of Illinois.

"The real problem, Mr. Vice President, may be where—in whose congressional district the second reburial takes place. The town where he was born believes he belongs there; the one where he graduated from high school thinks he's theirs. There's a memorial to him—a bodyless memorial as of now—in still a third place, where his regiment mustered. It was put there in 1866, right after the Civil War."

The vice president shook his head. "History has its imperatives, and so does politics."

The vice president then took Jim Allbritten's hand and said: "I was honored to be with you here today, Mr. Allbritten."

Jim Allbritten managed a tight smile as he mumbled a question about the vice president's well-known interest in the Civil War. Allbritten said he assumed it came from the vice president's being from the South—North Carolina?

"No, it began with my studying it at Benning in infantry school," said the vice president. "We each chose a battle to focus on—mine was Gettysburg."

The vice president had been a Green Beret officer in Vietnam, where he was wounded and won the Silver Star for valor, a fact that his ever-present lapel pin allowed no one to forget.

Fred Mackenzie, who, it seemed to Don, had barged his way into this small conversation group, said to the vice president: "The Civil War is part of our history here in East Preston. But it's not the passion for us, of course, that it is for you Southerners."

Jim Allbritten's animosity for Mackenzie was glaringly obvious. Before the vice president could respond, Allbritten said: "There is passion here for some of us."

The vice president misunderstood. "Certainly. This must be quite a relief to have your ancestor where he belongs—finally."

Fred Mackenzie remained silent but stood firm in the group around the vice president as if he belonged there.

Don wondered if the vice president knew any of the truth about what happened. Those involved in the Park Service and the Interior Department—including the vice president's political friend Mike Quinn—had taken a vow of silence. Whatever, the vice president was giving no hint of knowing anything.

But Don wanted to push Mackenzie away—literally shove this kin of a killer out of this circle. *Get out of here! You don't belong in this group with* us!

The vice president apologized for not being able to stay for the reception planned at the town hall across the green, and he disappeared into a black car and a motorcade for the short trip to his helicopter.

Don, Allbritten, and Mackenzie watched the vice president depart.

Then Allbritten pointedly turned away from Mackenzie, expressed his appreciation to Don, and began to leave.

Don was overwhelmed by the agony that consumed Jim Allbritten. Staring again at Allbritten's bleary, teary, crimson-rimmed eyes, Don had seen a 134-year-old demon seething in there. The past was in him. *And that's good, of course. It should be in all of us.*

"I wonder if I may speak to you for a moment?" Don called as he walked after Allbritten. It was said on reflex. He had to try to help this tormented man.

Jim Allbritten stopped, turned around. Mackenzie stepped forward to join them. Again, Don fought the impulse to push him away.

They were standing alone, the others having already moved on toward the postburial reception.

"Mr. Allbritten, I want you to know I understand and, in some ways, even share your distress." The words came out too stiff—too official.

Allbritten drew his mouth up as if he were going to spit—or scream. He did neither as he silently walked away, back toward the cemetery, away from the green and the reception. Don could feel an aura of hot anger in his wake.

Don took a step to follow Allbritten again, but Mackenzie held up his right hand to Don. "Leave it alone, Spaniel," he said, dropping the *Doctor* for the first time. "As we all know and the vice president said, there was horrendous confusion on that horrendous battlefield on that horrendous day. And now it is over."

Don wasn't so sure. His mind was racing with truly awful thoughts and images. But he didn't follow Jim Allbritten. Fred Mackenzie moved right up by him and joined in watching the slumping figure disappear into a scene of tall trees and graves.

"Jimmy's always hated me," said Mackenzie. "We competed for grades, for girls, for touchdowns and home runs and baskets, for student offices—now for clients, friends, influence."

"And you always win?"

"Not always—but usually. That's the story of the Mackenzies and the Allbrittens, I guess."

Don had to get away from here, from this man.

"You think Jimmy may kill me, don't you, Spaniel?" said Fred Mackenzie, dropping his voice to a wavering whisper. "Is that one of your historical imperatives?"

Don froze. "Do you deserve to die?" he whispered back.

"For something my great-great-grandfather did one hundred and thirty-four years ago? What do you think, Spaniel?"

Don made a tight, quick motion with his head. Fred Mackenzie could read it any damned way he chose.

"How do you think he'd do it?" Mackenzie's voice was still only a degree or two above a whisper.

Don, of course, knew exactly how it would happen. And his imagination rushed forward with precise images of Jim Allbritten killing Fred Mackenzie.

But, without a word, Don took off in a trancelike trot across the green toward the reception hall.

He paused after a few long strides to glance back, just in time to see Fred Mackenzie disappear into the scene of tall trees and graves.

Don had been in the hall for only a few minutes when he heard something above the crowd and noise of the citizens of East Preston. It startled him. Was it a gunshot?

"Couldn't be that," said a most unconcerned Doris Michelle Haynes, the mayor. "It's against the law to discharge any kind of firearm inside our town limits," she said with obvious pride.

She and Don were in conversation to the side of the refreshments table, barely away from the main crush of people who had come to celebrate the reburial of Kenneth Allbritten. The table offered unsweetened orange iced-tea punch and an array of colorful sweet pastries and tiny crustless sandwiches.

Don, before stopping to really talk, had made a quick trip around this common room in the town hall. It was clearly the center of the East Preston universe. Just inside, there was a large cork bulletin board full of tack-held notices for baby-sitters, meetings, yard sales, used bicycles, house and room rentals. Over a far door was a sign that said it was the place to go to pay the water bill and register to vote, among other governmental things. Against one wall was a dark mahogany horseshoe table where the town council did its business and listened to its populace. A good number of those folding chairs out on the green must have come from this room. The other walls were a gallery of unframed posters and scrawled artwork from schoolchildren and framed black-and-white historical photographs of East Preston.

Don and the mayor were talking about small-town life when the noise was heard. Don had just said how much he enjoyed living in Washington but, at the same time, often yearned for the pace and values of his hometown of Harrisonburg, Virginia.

"Somebody must have dropped something, that's all," said the burial service's Episcopal priest as he joined the twosome. "Made a bit of a bang, though, didn't it?" Don had not caught the clergyman's name earlier, and he missed it again now.

Don did not believe the sound was made by somebody dropping something.

"Where are Fred and Jim?" the priest asked the mayor. "This is more their party than anybody's."

The mayor said they would surely be here in a minute.

Don looked toward the door that led back out to the green. But he offered no report on the whereabouts or possible appearance times of Fred Mackenzie and Jim Allbritten.

Don then had a perverse fantasy upon spotting a microphone and loudspeaker system up in the town council's end of the room. He would go to the mike, make a call for attention, and shout: "Hear ye, hear ye, hear ye, good citizens of East Preston! Let the truth be known! Roland Mackenzie, great-great-grandfather of Fred Mackenzie, murdered Kenneth Allbritten on the seventeenth day of September at Antietam in the year of Our Lord eighteen hundred and sixty-two! Do you hear me, hear me, hear me, good citizens of East Preston?"

The priest said to the mayor: "It seems to me that this whole event has taken a toll on Jim. He seems extremely upset—nervous, at wit's end, so to speak. One would think he'd be pleased by all of this, wouldn't you, Doris?"

Don excused himself as if fulfilling an obligation to move about the room and meet more pleased East Prestonites. There were at least a couple of hundred people there, about as many as the room—even without any chairs—could handle. He moved quickly through a good number of them with smiles and handshakes and expressions of appreciation for their thanks to him for what he had done to bring Kenneth Allbritten home.

When he reached the door, he slipped outside onto the green.

There was the scene of the reburial—the chairs, the platform—now empty of people, sound, commotion, and purpose.

His nostrils caught the faint odor of burned gunpowder. Was it the smell of the Old Guard's rifle shots still in the air? Or was it something else—something fresher?

Don took off running toward the spot at the cemetery into which, one after another, Jim Allbritten and Fred Mackenzie had disappeared.

As with the soldiers, Don heard them before he saw them, some seventy-five yards into the cemetery, near its rear boundary, a rutted, dirt access road.

". . . and you lied about her then, and you've been lying about her ever since. . . ."

It was Allbritten's voice. There were sounds of grunts and scuffling.

Don stopped, froze.

He heard Allbritten again. "You've always lied about everything. You'd tell Coach Moultrie you'd run thirty laps when it was only twenty. You'd say you were the one who brought in the yard markers or the bases or the whatever after practice—when it was me or somebody else who did it. You'd say it wasn't *your* idea to change the play in the huddle when it was. You lied to your parents to get their car at night. You lied to me when you said you didn't understand trigonometry. Liar, liar, liar! That's what you are. Your great-great-grandfather lived a blood lie. It's in your blood. . . ."

There was more bustle and noise. Shouts and slaps. Cussing and sharp cries.

Don moved up behind a large tombstone, from where he could see as well as hear what was happening. He was about ten yards away now. He glanced at the marker. It was for a man named Jonathan Wendell Cooper, who according to the inscription was a "Much Loved Husband, Father and Physician" whose life spanned seventy-one years from 1875 to 1946.

Fred Mackenzie and Jim Allbritten were each a mess, their suits and shirts torn and dirty, their faces red and scarred. They had been in one helluva fight.

Two things were clear to Don. Allbritten was getting the best of it. And it wasn't over.

Allbritten said: "Go ahead, Freddy. Tell me how wrong I am, how I don't understand, how unfair it all is, what a shit I am for saying what I said about your lying, how sad it is that we aren't friends and haven't ever really been since Myra—"

Mackenzie threw his right fist. Allbritten's reflexes brought his own left arm up but only in time to deflect the blow to the side of his head. Allbritten, in angry reaction, rammed his fists, one after the other, hard into Mackenzie's stomach.

"Jesus . . ." Mackenzie said, bending over. "You want to kill me, don't you, Jimmy? You've been wanting to since Myra . . ."

Don blanched. *Kill? I'm going to stand here and watch one man kill another? Is that what I am going to do?*

Don didn't move.

Allbritten hit Mackenzie along the side of the head. And they grabbed each other in a clinch and fell hard to the ground.

They rolled over twice, stopping only after banging against a huge tombstone that had the name *Wollaston* engraved across the top.

My God, thought Don. *What am I doing reading the names off cemetery markers while these two men fight like this? I should do something. I should try to stop this.*

But he still didn't move.

Mackenzie and Allbritten rolled back the other way, first one on top, then the other. Mackenzie kicked Allbritten's left shin hard with the heel of his right shoe. Allbritten swore.

Then, suddenly, Mackenzie was on his feet. He was holding something in his right hand. Something he pulled out from under his coat.

It's a weapon. A revolver? Yes! Looks like a Colt .44. Yes! Must be the one from Mackenzie's office.

Mackenzie, holding it by the barrel end, swung the weapon down in a hammering motion. It made a cracking noise as it slammed against the top of Allbritten's head.

Jim Allbritten fell forward, spread-eagled on his stomach.

Don yelled, "No! Stop it! Enough!" and he lunged toward Mackenzie.

Mackenzie, his back to Don, didn't turn around. Instead, he leaned down, placed the barrel of the pistol against the base of Allbritten's skull.

Crack!

That was a gunshot. Before, it really must have been only somebody dropping something.

Don raced up to Mackenzie and shoved him aside as hard as he could. He looked down at Jim Allbritten. There was a huge gaping wound in the back of his head—blood and pieces of hair and skin were splattered on the back of his suit coat and on the ground on both sides of what remained of his skull.

Don, in horror, jerked from the sight on the ground to that of a sobbing Fred Mackenzie, the .44 Colt still in his right hand.

"Did you see what happened, Spaniel?" he cried.

Don did not answer.

Mackenzie's voice was raspy, frantic.

"There was a girl in law school. Jimmy loved her. There was a baby. He blamed me. It was twenty years ago. Ancient history. She lives in Texas, the baby's grown up, all is well. It's ancient history. . . ."

Don was unable to say anything. His mouth and his body would not—could not—move. Only his mind was in motion. Spinning, whirling, reeling.

This cannot be, cannot have happened. The imperative. What happened to the imperative? Allbritten had the score to settle, not Mackenzie. What must be, will *be.*

Mackenzie, the pitch of his voice rising, continued to speak in bursts.

"He was going to kill me. You said it yourself. I had no choice. It was him or me. That's why I took this gun with me today. I thought he might go crazy. You're my witness. It was self-defense. . . ."

Liar! It was cold-blooded murder! You executed him!

"You wanted Jimmy to kill me. Yeah, you did, Spaniel. You thought I had it coming. Because of what my great-great-grandfather did. That's nuts. You're nuts. I didn't kill anybody at Antietam. I didn't kill anybody anywhere anytime. Except just now. But this was self-defense. You saw it, didn't you, Spaniel?"

The words ricocheted off Don Spaniel. He tried to keep from listening, from hearing.

This was not the way it was supposed to end.

NOTES AND
ACKNOWLEDGMENTS

What you have just read is a work of fiction, but it is set in and around real events. There was a Civil War, of course, as well as a battle of Antietam, an Eleventh Connecticut, and a fight for a bridge that was later named after General Ambrose Burnside, who also existed. Kingsbury and Griswold and all but five of those mentioned from the Eleventh were real people who fought and/or died as they did here. The five nonreal ones were Allbritten and the four who killed and buried him. They, their hometown, and what they did that September 17 are complete figments of my imagination. So is Flintson of the Twenty-third Massachusetts, the lieutenant-messenger from Illinois, and all those involved in the present-day story. That means everyone from Womach and Spaniel, Milliken and Samuels, and Jim Allbritten and Fred Mackenzie to Rebecca Fentress, Colonel Doleman, and the vice president of the United States.

I tried to make the Civil War contexts for my fictional people and events as authentic as possible. The bibliography for this novel is contained within it, in fact. Every publication mentioned is real and so are the quotes, except those related directly to Allbritten, Mackenzie, Flintson, and those few others. For instance, the words Randolph uses in his confession to describe the horror on the battlefield are taken directly from real soldiers' first-person accounts in letters.

I had research assistance from a wide range of organizations, the most prominent being the National Park Service, the Smithsonian Institution, the U.S. Army Military Institute at Carlisle, the Connecticut Historical Society, and the library at Fort Myer, Virginia.

The individuals at those places and elsewhere to whom I am particularly indebted are: Richard Sommers, Kelly Nolin, Douglas Owsley, Paul Parvis, Jay Luvaas, David Umansky, Michael Heyman, Judy Fiscus, Sue Thompson, Darrell Dorgan, John Schildt, Susan Moore, Douglas Scott, Roger Kennedy, Dan Sagalyn, Annette Miller, and Amanda and Lew Nash.

I also want to thank the Civil War historians Ernest Furgurson, Richard Moe, and James Holland for their manuscript readings and reactions along the way. I owe thanks, too, to my editors at Random House, Susanna Porter and Bob Loomis, and to my friend and agent, Tim Seldes, to whom this book is dedicated.

I reserve a special appreciation for Stephen Potter, an archeologist for the National Park Service in Washington. He encouraged and guided me through this project from the very beginning. In fact, it was his work on some real Antietam remains, done with Doug Owsley of the Smithsonian, that helped trigger my initial interest.

And, while I am always dependent on the spiritual and editorial support I receive from my novelist wife, Kate, this time it truly made a decisive difference. Without her, this novel would never have seen the light of day.

Jim Lehrer

ABOUT THE TYPE

This book was set in Sabon, a typeface designed by the well-known German typographer Jan Tschichold (1902–74). Sabon's design is based upon the original letter forms of Claude Garamond and was created specifically to be used for three sources: foundry type for hand composition, Linotype, and Monotype. Tschichold named his typeface for the famous Frankfurt typefounder Jacques Sabon, who died in 1580.